# FABBLES: 1

Fabbles: 1
Copyright © 2013 by Hal Duncan
All rights reserved.

ISBN 978-1-291-64329-9

"A Scruffian Christmas" first published 2009 in a limited edition PDF ebook gift release for sponsors of The Scruffians Project. Commercially available for the first time here.

"The Beast of Buskerville" first published 2010 in PDF ebook edition via the author's website as part of The Scruffians Project.

"The Taking of the Stamp" first published 2013 in ebook edition from Popcorn, an imprint of La Case Books. Available on all major platforms.

Audio editions of "A Scruffian Christmas" and other Scruffians stories are available via the author's website at: www.halduncan.com. From the menu bar, select Take > Audio Downloads > MP3 Readings Service.

Contact the author at hal@halduncan.com to join the Scruffians mailing list, for news on future releases. Attach proof of purchase for FABBLES: 1 to recieve free PDFs of "A Scruffian Christmas" and "The Beast of Buskerville."

For more Scruffians fabbles, and sundry other tales of sprites and sodomites, see the forthcoming collection from Lethe Press, SCRUFFIANS!

Also available from the author:

VELLUM: THE BOOK OF ALL HOURS 1
INK: THE BOOK OF ALL HOURS 2
ESCAPE FROM HELL!
AN A-Z OF THE FANTASTIC CITY
SONGS FOR THE DEVIL AND DEATH

Forthcoming works:

SCRUFFIANS! (Lethe Press, April 2014)
TESTAMENT (TBA)
RHAPSODY (TBA)

New Sodom Press
www.halduncan.com

*To Michael*

# FABBLES: 1

## HAL DUNCAN

*Gor Bless Yer!*

*Hal Duncan*

New Sodom Press

# CONTENTS

A Scruffian Christmas            1

The Beast of Buskerville            9

The Taking of the Stamp            33

# A Scruffian Christmas

Twas the night before Christmas, and all through the workhouse not a creature was stirring... on account of any stirring'd most likely lead to a sound thrashing and a night in the mortuary, like, if the master heard a peep of it. No, if there'd been a mouse in the workhouse even he'd have kept his squeaker shut for fear of a master crueller than any cat. Not that a mouse could've lived off the crumbs in that workhouse, mind, where the paupers were eating the peelings for the pigs, and sucking the bones as they were grinding for fertiliser.

·

No, not one little waif in the kiddies' dormitories give even a snottery sob into a scrap of sleeve. They all knowed what anyone *ascertained to be an agitant* was in for, yeah? A guinea for a gamin, the overseers'd say. You mind yer manners and make yer money, or you'll be sold for a Scruffian, you hear? They'll put the Stamp on yer, Fix yer forever, and all ye'll be is meat in the machine!

They didn't know 'xactly what *Fixed* meant, the littl'uns—not like us what's had it done, eh, scamps?—but they knowed it was bad.

·

No, the Waiftaker General, he were as strange a story to them as Father Christmas. And the Institute—yeah, that Bad Place where he put the thingy on yer chest and it hurt summat hellish, then he cut yer pinky off and it grew right back—the Institute were as far away as the North Pole to them. *Indentured* means *enslaved*, they knowed. But they didn't know how the Stamp makes yer Scruffian, so's however yer starved or maimed by a master, well, ye'll always return to how yer Fixed. They just knowed enough to fear it.

Most of em.

·

See, there were one waif in the workhouse that Christmas Eve, and he were quiet as the rest of em—quieter even—but he were quiet in another way. Puckerscruff, you mind how Rake Jake Scallion looked as the stickmen carted him off to Newgate? All slyly smiling even in his chains, like it were all part of his plan? That were this unruffled lad as they led him to his bed and blanket. Oh, the soot that smeared every inch of him hid the look on his face a little, but them waifs saw the rebel in his eye.

·

A sweep's lad, so's his sad story went, when he turned up at the iron gates, bells ringing evenfall, night closing in, him shivering in the snow. A chimney-sweep's boy, only his master up and drinked himself to death, it being the season of celebrations. May the Good Lord punish this ungrateful wretch, sobs the urchin, but he'd *whip* me for saying my prayers, sir, even when I *blessed* him for his Christian charity. And now he's poisoned by gin, and I've nowhere to go, and… and…

Peter Black, he said his name was as they brung him in.

·

He's blessed, says they—leastways, there's a lot of *blessings* in their words—cause those iron gates was near locked for the night; a minute later and he would've been on a hiding to nothing. They don't hear him muttering how he's used to hiding and used to nothing; they's too busy ensuring his education in the *Christmas spirit* they're exemplifying, charitable Christians what they are, 'specially seeing as how it's well past supper and scrubbing-up time, with festive fun awaiting them as has *families* to be getting home to. Oh, they's most eloquent as regards his good fortune.

·

So now, here's this soot-covered sweep's lad, sat on a mouldy mattress, on a bed what stinks of the foundling as has recently vacated it, vacated the world in general, actually. Kicked into the room with a good-natured laugh and a gracious promise—breakfast and a good bath in the morning being, as they puts it, *the only gifts a filthy guttersnipe like you'll be getting, and be grateful even for that, wretch.* So here's he sits, this Peter Black, with all them other waifs laying in their beds but awake, peering at his shadow in the dark.

• 

When he stands up, they all starts to fret, like. When he walks to the window, they all sits up in their beds. When the floorboard under his foot gives a squeak, one of em's bold enough to hiss a shush at him, finger to his lips. There's panic in all of their eyes as the lad just smiles, his teeth so white in the pitch-black. Not one of em's brave enough to whisper him to stop though, as he fetches a match and a stub of candle from his ragged shirt, strikes the one and lights the other.

•

He moves the candle to the left, then to the right. He covers it with a hand, then he takes his hand away. Goes through this strange routine three times, so he does, before sauntering back to the middle of the room, cocky as can be, like as he'd have his paws in his pockets if his breeches only had em. Sets the candle down on the floor, yeah? Then sets himself down cross-pinned, with a glance of his glinting rebel eye around the room.

—Blimey, says he. I ain't never seen such timid tykes in all me natural.

•

—Hush! whispers one, his eyes as wide as a Whitechapel tart's snapper. The master'll hear yer and—

—It's Christmas Eve, says this saucy sweep's lad. Trust me, Tiny Timid, a Scruffian don't do nothing lest he's sure it's safe. Unless it's fun. Or he's got a good reason. Or leastways a reason. Well… never mind, in this here case, we's sent him a pressie—from the parishioners, so's he thinks. By now, the bugger should have polished off the port and be guggling out a glass of the finest brandy Lightfinger Larker ever half-inched. Laced with laudanum now, like.

•

Well, if there was ever a room of workhouse waifs as wonder-struck as them, I ain't never heard of it. Half of em was blowed over by the balls of this lad in speaking at all. Half of em was blowed over by that word what weren't *bleeder* or *blighter* or *blackguard*—and aimed at the workhouse master too, of all men! But half of em, all's they heard were the word *Scruffian* and that struck fear into their hearts. Why, if their ears weren't deceiving em, if they weren't bonkers to even believe in Scruffians, this were one!

•

—You're a Scruffian? whispers one.

—What's a Scruffians? hisses another.

—Is it true? asks a third. Is it true they cuts yer soul out and puts it in a box and then even fire can't burn yer and—

—Nah, most of that's a load of bollocks, says the lad. But come cosy up round this here glim and I'll show yer what I am.

And as he says this, he reaches his hand inside his shirt, stretching right round the back and down, as if to get summat tucked into his breeches. And out comes his hand holding a shiv.

•

The first waif comes tiptoeing timorously from his bed as our lad takes the edge of that shiv to the wrist of his left fam, cuts deep enough to spurt. The second and third come creeping, silent, as he puts that hand to his chest, starts rubbing at the soot there, using that squirting blood to wet and wipe the black. More of em come then, horrified by the gory muck, by the fact he's washing it crimson now. All of em's crowded round by the time's he wipes the blood off with his shirt, to show em the Stamp.

•

Even streaked with blood, now's the soot's gone it ain't hard to see the scars on him, criss-crossing this way and that, circling and spiraling, like the strangest script written in his skin. It's who he is, what's writ on him, says he, stamped into his flesh to Fix him forever. He was once a workhouse waif like them. He stops a second, gives a queer little smile, sorta sad. In a way, he *is* a workhouse waif like them, he says. Always will be.

—Still. It has it's perks, says he.

He holds up a wrist already healed.

•

As them waifs all sit in awe, he clambers to his pins, saunters to the door. He tells em to wait here for… half an hour or so, he reckons. Shouldn't take too long to sneak his way through the workhouse, do what has to be done. He don't say what that is, but his impish grin and the wink he tips em says it's all in the name of festive fun.

—Bless yer sweet souls, says he. It's a crime as waifs should want at Christmas.

Then off he slips, so softly, quiet as a thief in the night.

•

They waits then, the waifs. They waits for *minutes* and *minutes*. Ain't none of em as can imagine what might be in store, but every one of em is whipped up to whispers, and counting those minutes, the seconds, the beats of their hearts. Why, if it ain't a true Christmas Eve for em! All the anticipation they ain't never had before, on a night as only ever minded em of their motherless misery! One nipper peers out the window, pipes up that the gates is open now. Whatever could be happening?

—Come see, says the Scruffian at the door.

•

Now he leads em out the room. They're terrified at first, thinking what if the master catches em out, what if there's an overseer about, what if, what if! But our black-faced Scruffian seems so sure as he struts ahead that it ain't too long before their whispers become murmurs, and their murmurs become chatter, and their chatter becomes excited. And there's another Scruffian leading the girls from *their* dormitory. And they're all babbling chipper as chaffinches, like life'd never ground em down at all, as they piles into the refectory. And they hushes.

—Grub's up, says the Scruffian.

•

Now, us Scruffians learn to live with starving, Fixed with hunger in our bellies. It's a cruel thing, innit? Cause even when yer have a bang up feast—like what we had after yer liberation, mind, when Flashjack and

Joey sprung yer from the Institute?—well it's barely over than yer tummy's torturing yer again. But it works both ways for us, that hunger Fixed so's it can't get worse. But think how's it is for them waifs what's *wasting*, wasting to the *grave* as the workhouse master gobbles up his roast goose. Maybes yer might even mind that misery.

•

Well, that's why, when them waifs walked into the refectory, well, most of em near wept for joy, cause what did they see but a score of Scruffians with pots of stew, and pies, and sausages—and was that rashers of bacon all piled up on a plate, and another with—could it be?—roast ham? Oh, the smell of that roast ham, it filled the very air! There weren't much in the way of veg, like, but bollocks to veg when there's meat on the table, eh? Meat, meat and more meat! They hadn't never seen such a thing!

•

I tell yer, there were a few of the Scruffians as didn't have dry eyes themselves, watching them tykes tuck in, smiling proudly whiles they nibbled on a sausage themselves or munched on a pie. It's a glorious feeling to give such a gift; that's why we does it, sore as it is on us.

What's that, scamp?

Every year. Different workhouse, natch. They tends to up the security afters, but they has to hush it up, cause they knows it's us. Can't exactly blab to the Bow Street Runners, fingering them as they sold for Scruffian slaves. Not *officially*.

•

Oh, but the best is still to come. Yeah, stick that in the pot, scamp; good lad. No, Flashjack, not *that*. Scrape the meat off it for the sausage mince; don't want no bones in the stew. Where was I? Yeah, the best bit of the story! Cause that feast were only for Christmas Eve, to fill the bellies of them ravenous ragamuffins, give em a taste of happiness, so's they'd meet the morning with smiles on their faces. Grub as a gift's all fine and dandy, but bollocks to getting what yer *need* for Christmas. That's just shite, eh?

•

So, by some happy coincidence of timing—what might *seem* unlikely and invented, if one was a sour-faced sodding scofflaw as picks holes in stories, *Joey*—by some fluke of fate, as it happened, the last morsel of meat got its last munch in a waif's mouth, and was swallowed down on the very moment that, out in the cold, December night, Bow Bells began to chime.

—Well, blow me! says that black-face Scruffian. Why, it's never…
And as all the waifs look round at him, he grins.
—It ain't never *midnight*, is it? That means…
—MERRY CHRISTMAS!

•

And fuck me up the cracker with a stickman's cosh if the voice that bellows out that Yuletide blessing don't belong to none other than Bold Nick Scantilaw. The oldest Rake what ever lived, and the most Scruffian of em all, for all his size and shape, a true Scruffian in his heart. Bold Nick Scantilaw, Fixed in his infirmity, fatter than Falstaff and fine with that. Oh, he's a jolly old soul, with his beard and belly, his robes as red as the robin's breast. When the stickmen's bloodstains are fresh, that is. Mostly they're sorta reddish-brown, like.

•

—MERRY CHRISTMAS! says he. Why, the night I've had, bashing in the brains of blackguards who'd sell waifs into slavery, ripping out the hearts of the rich and ruthless who'd buy em, lopping off limbs of factory-owners who'd throw scamps and scrags into the grinding gears. Oh, the stickmen are trembling in their beds tonight, my foundlings and furies! Bold Nick's hellion crew's abroad, and the Waiftaker General himself wouldn't dare show his face on *my* streets. You can call me a fool, but I'm king for the night! This night is mine, and I call it MERRY CHRISTMAS!

•

And out he swaggers among the wide-eyed waifs, hauling presents from the sack unslung from his shoulder. Here's a locket as once belonged to your mother, says he to one. And this wipe was swiped across your father's brow, he says to another. This fob watch was your Uncle Jake's, says he to a third. You didn't *know* you had an Uncle Jake? he says. Ho ho *ho!* My boy, you *did*, and he *so* wanted you to have this.

Why, Bold Nick Scantilaw has gifts for all—better still, pressies only truly precious to them as gets em.

•

You should've seen the smiles on those waifs' faces, scamps. A beauty to behold, it were. Well, ye'll see it tonight. He always has pressies for the Scruffians too, you know, maybes a tarnished trinket, maybes the gaudiest gold, but always summat as only *you* would truly cherish. Where do he get them? He's Bold Nick Scantilaw! He takes em back, from them powerful privileged fuckers as prised em from their rightful place.

What? *Of course* they really belonged to them waifs' folks. Give me this very ticker last year, what I played with on me grandad's knee. Gob's truth!

•

Well, there ain't much more to tell than that, really. Bold Nick Scantilaw, he gives out them pressies, but he has to be offsky after, sharpish like, cause it's Christmas, and that ain't the only workhouse in the world, eh? And the Scruffians, they has to be offsky before the stickmen or the traps come. And the waifs? Well, we offers em to come with us if they wants, but ain't more'n a handful of em ever does. Ain't like it's that much safer being an *escaped* slave, on the streets. No, most're happy with just having had… a Christmas.

•

See, it's the *giving* as matters, scamps. Course, ain't much yer can give when ye've got fuck all yerselves; really, all's we've got to give em *is* ourselves. But us Scruffians can give plenty of that, right?

Yeah, I know it hurts, but it'll grow back. See? The stumps already sprouting. And don't the stew taste *scrummy?* Now, you trot offsky, go get yer shivs from Flashjack.

Psst, Joey. How's that Scantilaw costume coming along?

*Yes,* you have to. Yer the only one as can do the voice. And you loves it anyways.

Besides, it wouldn't be Christmas without Scantilaw.

# The Beast of Buskerville

• 1

The Beast of Buskerville? Now there's a tale! Why, it's only the tale of old Whelp, eh? The tale of the most frightsome hound as ever haunted London, and of Yapper, the Scruffian as learned to speak Dog, the Scruffian as *tamed* Whelp... well, as near to tamed him as that snarling, slavering, scurrilous cur of a canine ever could be tamed. But more'n that, scamps, this here's a tale of the single most villainest villain ever to prey on the likes of us, the vulture of vagabonds, the buzzard of beggars, the scavenger of Scruffians... the Waiftaker General himself.

•

Now, you all's seen the Waiftaker General with yer own peepers, so there ain't no need for conjuring him, right? Back when this story took place, he'd the same beak nose of a bird of prey, the same beady eyes with pinprick pupils, the same scrawny neck to angle his head this way and that, to size up a Scruffian just Fixed or all set for a Scrubbing. Only thing different back then... though his hair it were slicked back to his skull the same, so's he looks a true hawk—back then it were black instead of white.

•

So. It began on a day as seemed like any others for the Waiftaker General, as he rose from his fancy four-poster bed, bid his butler hold the piss-pot for him whiles he drains his bladder, then pour water—piping hot!—for him to wash his fams. Why, that butler even buttons up his breeches, he does; helps him on with his big black frockcoat what flaps like wings when he pounces on yer; and knots his white silk cravat so *sartorially sophisticated...* what only makes his neck look scrawnier, poking out as a vulture's from its ruff.

•

All the whiles he were dressing, of course, he were already at work, calling in his lieutenant to tell him how many waifs was took for Fixing in the dead of night, and was they Jews or gypsies, paupers or carnies? Was they boys or girls with black mops or blond curls? What ages and stages of starving was they? So what was their worth at the going rates? And all of this writ in his little black book. And then lastly he spins, with a smile cruel as sin, and asks, How many *scruffs* did the stickmen bring in?

• 2

Now on this day, after all these accountings of the night's business, there's a few more things for the Waiftaker General to be asking after, yeah? This weren't no different from no other day, mind, cause he'd always have what he calls *extraordinary business.* One day it might be a partic'lar Scruffian as is vexing him sorely with spritely shenanigans—Lightfinger Larker outdoing himself as prince of the pickpockets, or Flashjack Scarlequin playing scourge of the stickmen. Others it might be *truly* extraordinary—rascalry from Rake Jake Scallion or some other Rake as *looks* like a groanhuff but's Scruffian inside.

•

Today though, it were the Beast of Buskerville to be dealt with, and for some reason—a reason what nobody in all his staff knew, not his butler nor his lieutenant, nor one of his stickmen, nor a single sausage in all the lodges across London—this partic'lar *extraordinary business* did seem to get the Waiftaker General's feathers extraordinarily ruffled. What news of the Beast of Buskerville? he snapped, soon as the tally of snaffled scofflaws was noted. Is there sight or sound of it? Sniff of spoor of it? What news of that bothersome, blackguardly brute of a Beast?

•

See, there ain't no borough more troublesome to the stickmen than Buskerville anyways, on account of it having its streets *all over* London, it being patched from the pitches of all em organ-grinders, penny-whistlers, Punch-and-Judy-men and whatnots. Worse, it's always on the move, always shifting, and that's a thing as no stickman can stand. Can't get their heads round it, can they? Course, every Scruffian knows Buskerville the way a sailor knows knots; there's rich pickings to be made among the toffs as dawdle on its corners, wipes and tickers just waiting to be plucked.

•

So if there was anywheres in London as caused the Waiftaker General grief, it were Buskerville; and lately that Buskerville botheration had gotten sorer still, with reports of routs—panic in the streets—all sparked by vicious attacks from a dread fiend of the four-legged faithful-friend variety. Nobs was being savaged, and their brats was being mauled, by some demon dog as like to go for a throat as for a toffee apple. A demon dog, says they, as had been shot, stabbed, scorched, you name it, and weren't nothing could keep it killed. Could it possibly be…?

• 3

—A Scruffian dog? says the Waiftaker General as he steps down from the carriage that's took him all the way from his Kensington townhouse to his Westminster workplace, that dark, domed crematorium of a construction they calls the Institute. Perhaps, he says as he swipes his cane at some hawker stood on the steps with a lad on a leash—an urchin to be Fixed, no doubt, and an owner as needs learning in the protocols of propriety, to bring his purchase to the *appropriate* entry.

—Perhaps, he says to the lieutenant as scurries after him. Perhaps some… failed experiment.

•

—An investigation must be instigated, of course, says he. An inquiry must be initiated, an inquest inaugurated. If this monstrous mongrel is indeed a product of our hallowed Institute, why, this is a scandalous misuse of our facilities. Scandalous! Tell the PM he may rest assured: we *will* uncover the culprit of this crime, and deal with him severely. *Most* severely.

Oh, there was a black scowl in the Waiftaker General's beady eyes as he says those words. There's few groanhuffs can brood as bitter as the Waiftaker General, foul-tempered fucker that he is.

—Heads *will* roll, says he.

• 

—But of course, says he as he aims another swipe at the hawker (who don't seem to be fathoming the correctitude of conduct as is being imparted to him through the medium of whacking, who's still worrying at the sleeve of the lieutenant as is s'posed to open the Institute's front doors for Himself, holding him back from doing his dutiful.) Of course, says the Waiftaker General, our priority of primacy must be the apprehension of this foul abomination, the extermination of this vile vermin, the Scrubbing of this Scruffian canine. If indeed that is the nature of this… this…

•

Oh, there was a right sour twist to the Waiftaker General's thin lips as he spoke. Might have been a slight bite to em too, me scamps, the bite of lip on a man as wants to say more than he ought to, a villain as has an awful urge to rant and rail, but has a damn good reason not to blather his bile too wildly, eh? But if there were, it wasn't such as the lieutenant were like to notice with the hawker tugging at his sleeve and Himself exploding:

—The side-entrance, you cretinous oaf, he shouts.

• 4

Now, that were the first the Waiftaker General truly noticed the nature of this hawker as was harrying his man. And if ever there was anything made to revolt him to the depths of his soul—anything as wasn't an escaped Scruffian, that is—it was this pitiful peddler. Hunchbacked and hook-nosed, he was, a Rumpelstiltskin as rag'n'bone man, wearing the black-glassed spectacles of the blind, with straggly hair and matted beard as might be grey or even white underneath all the filth. Togged in tatters too, layer upon layer. And the sight weren't nothing to the stench.

•

But now as the Waiftaker General had actually noticed the peddler, he couldn't help but notice the urchin what was with him too; and if the peddler had him wanting to wash the filth from the Institute's front steps with a firehose, why, that boy made him wants to purge it with purifying flames first, for he'd never seen no Scruffian as scruffy as this in all his puff. Barely clothed, the boy was, in rags as hardly kept him decent, the number of holes they had in em. Why, the dirt made a better job of covering his flesh.

• 

More'n that though, the Waiftaker General, he saw then that this weren't no urchin being brung for Fixing, but a Scruffian already Fixed, the scars of the Stamp upon his chest for all to see, under his buttonless shirt, when the boy sat back on his haunches—as he did just at that moment. He weren't just on a leash that lad, see, a leather collar round his neck and a chain held tight in the peddler's liver-spotted hand; he even walked on all fours like a dog, sat down like one too, at a yank of his leash.

•

Now the Waiftaker General weren't inclined to be intrigued by this. Was he bollocks! No, all the more reason for him to rail at this noisome nuisance, cause Scruffians to be Scrubbed *definitely* wasn't for the front doors. But with him proper noticing the hawker now, well, nows he noticed what the man were saying. And that *were* intriguing.

—If ye please, yer vorshipful 'onour, says this hunchback hawker. My name is Lionel J. Reakesack, and fer all as I'm blind and beggarly, yer eminent regality, I'm come here with me Scruffian to 'elp yer catch the Beast of Buskerwille.

• 5

There's wicked and cruel men who would have simply laughed then, scoffed at the notion of such scum being of service, being useful in any manner other than maybes keeping rats in check by hunting em for mealtime morsels. But that's a kind of wicked and cruel as has a sense of humour in all its nastiness, and the Waiftaker General, he ain't even got that to be said for him. Ain't never so much as a snigger passed those lips, not a chortle nor a chuckle. So all's he done was sneer down the beak of his cocked snoot.

• 

—To help us catch the Beast of Buskerville? says he. And just how does a piddling peddler such as you, an aptly-named *reeking sack* of misshaped penury such as you, propose to be of assistance? You do understand that as the Waiftaker General I have the entire Institute at my disposal, not to mention the constables of every lodge across the whole of London? How precisely do you fancy yourself, a blind cripple, facillitating the capture of that cur?

—If ye please, yer esteemed reverence, says Reakesack. If ye please, I've come to offer me serwices as a tracker.

•

—Well, in truth, says he, if ye please, yer magnanimous magnificence, it ain't so much *my* serwices that I'm enwisioning as may be of some walue; no, it's the serwices of me Scruffian 'ere. Now, blind as I am, I can't see yer scorn, but as a certainty I can imagine it, sir; for sure and this creature must look as vorthless to you as to the sot I bought 'im from; and truth be told that drunk had so little use for 'im I got the lad for a bottle of gin. Got 'im to be me eyes, sir.

•

—But ye see, says he, if yer please, yer resplendent nobilitude, the boy were a vild child, found in a forest or summat, never learned to talk nor even walk upright. Fixed for to be a guard dog, growling being 'is only apparent skill. Veren't much use at that neither; 'e's a craven whelp as cowers at a kick—see? Oh, but bless the good Lord if old Lionel J. Reakesack didn't find a use for a boy raised as a dog, and not just as me eyes. As me nose too, sir. Oh, my Yapper'll *sniff out* yer Beast.

• 6

Now the Waiftaker General hadn't never heard of no feral child being Fixed, but old Reakesack 'splained as the lad were from way back, according to the sot what owned him afore. Guarded the family business for generations, stretching back to the days of his grandfather's grandfather, so he says. Kept with the dogs for a century or more, until he come to think he was one, even come to know his way by his nose just like a dog. Course, then that sot drunk away that family business, and what use were a guard dog with nuffink to guard?

•

—Now mark me, says Reakesack, for I'll not lie to ye, yer blessed grace; it's a fishy story, of a truth, if ye please. For as ye see when I kicks 'im—see?—or when I smacks 'im with 'is leash—see?—or even if I just clips 'is ear—see?—he don't growl at *nothing*. So I reckon as that sot was spinning a yarn and thinking to pull a fast one on old Lionel J. Reakesack. But bollocks to that bugger, hee hee, if ye'll pardon me French, for I got the best of 'im in the end.

•

—A Scruffian vot ain't got no words to be always asking questions, says Reakesack. A dog vot 'as the smarts to answer. Yes and no. Two yaps for yes, and one yip for no. Ain't that right, boy?

And blimey if that boy didn't give two little yaps in answer.

—Ye'll be a good dog for yer master, won't yer, boy? says Reakesack.
—Yap yap, says the lad.
—Knows the Beast of Buskerwille's stink, don't yer, lad?
—Yap yap.
—Yer can sniff yer way to 'is lair, boy, can't yer?
—Yap yap.
—And ye'll not lead us astray, eh?
—Yip.

•

So the Waiftaker General he peers at the scamp, angling his head this way and that; and the scamp he's just sat there, tongue lolling from his mouth. Then he peers at old Reaksack, angling his head that way and this; and old Reaksack *he's* just stood there, tongue licking at his lips. The gleam of guineas in his eyes, he has, thinks the Waiftaker General, the greedy grubbing avarice of a right Jew.

Oh, but the Waiftaker General, he has his own hunger rising in his heart. It just ain't wealth he's wanting.

The Waiftaker General, he wants *blood*.

—Look sharp! he snaps at his lieutenant. Sound the bell! I want ten men, with pistols, nets and ropes, here *now*! Go on! he roars. I want them ready for the hunt, ten of the best, snapped to attention, spick and span—you know I'll stand no less—and if this blistering breath has ended by the time they're here, by God, if I have time to catch another breath to blast, I swear my next will signify your last, I'll have your badge, your balls, and all the seed they've sown, you laggardly, lollygagging, lazy…
 —Very good, he says.

•

So there's a baker's dozen of em as sets out in search of the Beast—the lieutenant counting himself as one of the best, natch—an unlucky thirteen of em, as they might have had good sense to pay some mind to: ten broke-nosed, brawny stickmen with coshes, all dolled up like a boxer's wedding party in their grey bowlers and tin flutes; the Waiftaker General at the head of em, his topper on tight, his cane tapping sharp with his stride; Reakesack up front, scurrying on, stoop-shouldered; and this lad, half-pauper, half-pup, leading the pack.

•

They starts the hunt in Covent Garden, where's many a Scruffian snaffles treats and trinkets; though there ain't many a Scruffian in sight soon as em stickmen stride in. Why, one whistle from a lad sat watching Jack Ketch hanging Punch, and half the audience is offsky in a flash, scattered into the mob like mouses to their holes, and scarper signals by the score sounding all through the market. But for once the beak-nose bastard ain't a-flap and screaming shrill, to *grab em* and *nab em*. Oh, no; it ain't scruffs is on the Waiftaker General's mind today.

•

—This… marketplace, says he, voice dripping with disdain of all em flower-girls and fruit-hawking costermongers. The last sighting of the Beast was in this… vicinity, was it not?
 —Indeed, sir, says his man. Last night, no less, stealing sausages from

some servant's—

—How most like a Scruffian, sneers the Waiftaker General. Well, Reakesack, set your whelp to work; and pray it does as promised, else…

—Of course, yer 'igh-born 'oliness, says Reakesack.

And down he bends to pinch the lad's ear, hiss his orders in it, seal em with a curse and cuff.

And then they's off.

• 8

At first they ain't going nowhere fast, Yapper leading em in circles, snuffling at the stalls and cobblestones, wandering left and right to weave his way amongst the mob of serving-maids with shopping baskets and whatnot. First it's all zig-zags and criss-crossings, now this way, now that, like as that lad were scribbling out the very Stamp scarred in his chest, in all its convolutions. 'Fore long though, Yapper, he's straightening out to sniff his way along one wall, stopping to cock his head. Then with an almighty howl, that Scruffian lad starts straining at his leash.

•

Out of Covent Garden he pulls em, scrabbling keen along the kerbs, up Bow Street and around, down Drury Lane, with all its plate-glass-windowed gin palaces—and there's more'n one rogue there eyes em stickmen as they pass, pipe in his teeth, hand drifting to them scars he never shows nobody—his Stamp. There's more'n one Rake gives a queer peer at Reakesack in partic'lar. And slinks back into a doorway as the Waiftaker General marches past.

Along and around, nipping down this alley here, this back-street there, off Kingsway and back on it, Yapper leads em.

•

Every turn as can be took along High Holborn, Yapper takes it, and some more besides, winding wigglier than the Thames itself, and never tiring, so it seems, even as morning passes into afternoon, even as the proud stride of the Waiftaker General and his stickmen gets less puffed-up and more puffed-*out* what with all em hours of walking. It's early-afternoon afores they even reach the Old Bailey, mid-afternoon by the time they's jostling through the crowds of Cheapside, Reakesack casting glances at the glint of signet rings and scarf pins in the jewellers' shop-windows.

•

As the afternoon stretches on, Yapper starts to lead em north, he does, up through Petticoat Lane with all its stalls of clobber top-notch or tatty; and the Waiftaker General he scowls at the traders with their sidelocks and wide-brimmed hats, mutters about immigrants and churches turned to synagogues. On and up they goes, more directly now, as evening sets in, using bluster and bullying to carve a clear path through Spitalfields Market as the traders is closing up their stalls for the night. Up to the edge of Bethnal Green and Shoreditch.

To the Old Nichol Rookery.

• 9

—Of course, says the Waiftaker General as Yapper halts, starts whining, cringing from the kicks what Reakesack aims to send him on, but stubborn as an animal as smells its own death in the abbatoir ahead. Tain't no abbatoir as is in front of em, that loverly little neighbourhood marked out by Half Nichol Street and Boundary Street, Old Nichol Street and Nichol Row, that cesspit of a slum owned by the pious and rented to the poor, three families to each house. Tain't no abbatoir, but it might as well be, how it treats em animals as enters it.

•

—Gerron, yer warmint! snarls Reakesack, whipping his Scruffian forward with the chain.

—A most suitable habitation for a mongrel scruff, says the Waiftaker General as he brings out his pistol. On your guard, men.

Into the lair of the Beast they goes then, into the rookery's maze of blackened tenements, more'n a score of narrow streets, all reeking with the stench of tripe and tallow, cow's shit and cat's meat, dead dogs' corpses in the mud. Dark doorways gape on either side, doors long-since gone for firewood. Eyes peer at em through broken soot-smeared windows.

In they goes.

•

Three men the Waiftaker General sends down a side-street, to circle round. Three men he orders down another alley as might hide a hound Three he sends off yet another way entirely, three in each team cause even pairs ain't safe in the Old Nichol, not even the beefiest bruiser stickmen, with the heftiest coshes they can carry. But yer don't catch nothing in the Old Nichol lest ye can box it in. So they needs to be smart, he tells them, leave the Beast nowheres to run.

—Sound your whistle if you see it, men, says he. Immediately.

•

Course, with old Reakesack and his Scruffian hardly counting in a scrap, well, the Waiftaker General, all's he's got is his lieutenant now, but he ain't one to be trembling with no stickmen at his side. Don't you be fooled by all his fineries into thinking he's a fop. Don't you be thinking, as he's heartless, why, he must be gutless too. Evil don't come so neatly wrapped, me scamps, all tied up with a dainty ribbon. No, that there waiftaker were a man with ice in place of blood, a man as hadn't *never* known fear.

Until that day.

• 10

On through the rookery they goes, eyes watching em all the way, children and drunks being dragged in off the streets, quarrels cut-off with fists at faces, songs stilled to silence halfways through a verse, *all* ruckuses dying in their path, like as the Angel of Death has come to Egypt, come to take their firstborn. Men as would murder for a sniff what slighted em steps back to let the vulture of vagabonds pass.

Only once had a Waiftaker General come to grief in any London slum. Tales is still told of the tithe took by his heir.

•

Sudden and sharp, a sound cuts through the air—a whistle! Off to the west it is, and the Waiftaker General's after it in a jiffy, pistol in the air— Come on! This way down an alley, that way now, he runs, the slap of steps echoing off the walls as the whistle blows again, then cuts off dead. He's still running when another whistle sounds—to the south now.

—Quick! It's on the move!

A third whistle! This time to the north—too far away, surely. He whirls, coat billowing, his lieutenant stumbling not to run right into him.

•

Now the second whistle blows again, no more'n yards away; he sprints to a corner, pistol aim sweeping round at… nothing. Another whistle! The first again? But to the east now? How? And he ain't barely off his mark—the lieutenant, Reakesack and Yapper in tow—when a shrill tin shriek sounds far behind. Now all three whistles sounds at once, here, there and elsewheres, notes drawn long, and longer still, going on and on until… they stops.

All's silence.

Silence except for Yapper's whimper as he slinks back, cowering, quivering, peepers fixed on the black maw of a doorway.

•

—Sir, says the lieutenant. Sir! The Scruffian!

The Waiftaker General, he's got the gears of his noggin whirling right now, figuring how's the rookery scum's called a reckoning upon themselves by ambushing his men, interfering in his extraordinary business; but he's quick to catch the drift of his lieutenant's fluster. The hawker ain't slow neither, finger pointing.

—Is 'e in there, boy? says Reakesack.

—Yip!

—'E's in there, sir! The Beast!

In the Waiftaker General's noggin, a tiny niggle—*yip*, one *yip*—catches a cog only to be whirled away. No matter.

At last the Beast is within his grasp.

• 11

The Waiftaker General goes in first, pistol in one hand, cane in the other. His lieutenant follows, cosh and net at the ready. Ain't a flicker of light in the tenement close. Only hints of gloaming seeps through the cardboard and rags what patches a window on the stairwell, halfways up to the first floor. Ain't no lights in the ground floor flats neither, nor a peep of human habitation. In a rookery as has folks living twenty to an home.

—Search them, sir? asks the lieutenant.

The Waiftaker General points at where Yapper's nosing.
—Up the stairs, says he.

•

On the first floor landing, it's darker still, without even the light from the close's front door. They peers into flats with windows boarded up, but all's they make out is rotten floorboards smeared with filth they smells more'n sees. Up to the second floor they goes, into deeper blackness, like as someone's sealed up every crack what might let in the slenderest shaft.

—Ah, vait just a tick, yer grandiose vorthiness, says Reakesack. I've a glim here, sir, I'm sure. Hold this.

He gives the lieutenant the leash, rummages out a candle, strikes a light, a phosphorous flash, and—

•

Of a sudden, Yapper barks and bolts, leash spinning the lieutenant like a top, yanking him round and off-kilter even as it's ripped from his grip. The lieutenant stumbles, snapping a curse that's killed in his throat by a black shape shooting from a doorway. Then the match is dropped, it's snuffed, and the afterlight in their peepers makes the darkness worse. All's they hear is the savaging, the gurgling screams, the thumping and thrashing. There's another flash, with a bang this time—the buzzard's pistol—but it's wild, shook by Reakesack clutching at the arm, screaming, mercy! mercy!

•

—Damn you, man! Let go!

The Waiftaker General clubs the peddler with his cane, struggles free to fire another half-aimed shot at the sounds of horror, gets a glimpse of eyes and teeth and blood. He falls back as it hits him, feels the cane thrash in his grasp, hears the hound's blood-curdling wrath in his face, smells its breath, feels its slaver. He don't hardly know what he's doing as he shoots and swings, and rolls and shoots. Then the cane's torn from his grasp, but he feels the lieutenant's net beneath him, grabs it, flings it.

Now there's something on him again, but it's Reakesack, panicked to a wild and howling scrabble, like as he wants to get up on his shoulders and behind his back all at once. And now the pistol's knocked from his hand, and it's the Waiftaker General's turn to howl in rage, not a string of curses at the bloody Beast and peddler, the accursed darkness and damned chaos, just a single wordless bellow of wrath. He's no fool to be lost to his ire though, not that vulture. He's already figuring where the Beast is from its snarl and struggle.

•

He throws Reakesack off him, stumbles back, hand slapping on a rickety banister that near collapses with a mighty crack under his weight. Yes! With a roar he slams himself into it, splintering wood. Now he rips out a balustrade for a bludgeon, throws himself at the shape in the shadows, wild as some monstrous ape. The rotted wood shatters in his hand, but there's bone cracks too, he's sure, from the hellish yowl as the Beast gives out. Tain't even nearly down and out though, and its lurching brings it twixt him and the way out down the stairs.

•

But the peddler's already sorted *his* solution to that, fleeing past the Waiftaker General, screaming as he goes.
 —Upstairs! Upstairs! Follow the Scruffian!
 And it's near drowned out by the Beast, but sure enough Yapper's frantic yelping can be heard above. The Waiftaker General, he don't stop to think, knows that the Beast ain't more'n stunned, that he has to fall back, find a weapon, higher ground. He turns, leaps the stairs three at a time, spots light ahead of him now—yes!—on the landing, from a flat, a room, an open door—snarling at his heels—a door!

•

And he's in, with the door slammed shut at his back, the Beast pounding into it on the other side, shuddering it, a demon crazed with hunger for his blood. But he's safe. A chair sits just beside the door, and he hauls it round, jams its back tight under the handle. He looks round the room for anything else as might help his barricade, but all he sees is Reakesack panting and the Scruffian...

He sees the Scruffian stood at a bare brick fireplace, leaning on the Waiftaker General's cane, spinning his leash, and grinning, casual as can be.

• 13

There ain't many as has had the Waiftaker General lost for words, but Yapper he got that bugger gawping like a goldfish. It might have been him nicking the bastard's own cane, and it might have been him playing dandy with his own chain, but I likes to think it were mostly just the sight of Yapper standing on his own two feet as dumbfounded the Waiftaker General. Whatever it were, the buzzard were so blowed over, it were Yapper had to speak first.

—One yip *always* means yes, says he.
—Reakesack? growls the Waiftaker General.
—Yer hubristicality? sneers Reakesack.

•

Now as the peddler strolls over to stand beside Yapper, the Waiftaker General looks around a room as is empty of aught but that one chair holding back the slavering Beast. Floorboards and fireplace is all there is, and windows with ragged-edged grills nailed, screwed and bolted over em, crude but crafted for a purpose as is all too obvious. A cage, he thinks.

—Reakesack, I swear—
—He ain't the one to be swearing at, says the Scruffian.
Oh, how the Waiftaker General glowered at that. The filthy *scruff*...
—You, he says. Who do you think you are that—?

•

—Yer don't *really* has to know my name or story, says Yapper. Fact, yer don't *get* to know my story. All's yer need know is that I'm awful fond of dogs. Ain't a dog in the world that's not a little bit Scruffian in its heart, so *all* us Scruffians loves our poochy pals, yeah? But even me crib-mates says I'm downright daft for me mongrel mates. So what? says I. So what if

I likes to go down to all the strays in the backstreet bivouacs and feed em any grub as I've got spare? It's mine, innit?

•

—So what, says I, if this Beast of Buskerville everyone's gabbing about is fiercer than a ticked-off tiger? I talk Dog, don't I? Tain't that hard if yer lives with em for long enough; it's mostly *feed me* and *bad men* and *cats!* Anyways, if it's true that Beast's been Fixed, says I, ain't we obliged to offer it a crib? So I had a little shufty for him, yeah? Took yonks to find him, but in the end…

—Blow me if he ain't indeed a Scruffian dog, says Yapper. A Scruffian dog! But you already knows that, eh?

• 14

The Waiftaker General glowers at him then, saying nuffink with his lips but blathering the bleeding works of Charlie Dickens in the glare of his murderous peepers. A Scruffian dog and he knows it alright. Blow me if he ain't got the look all em groanhuffs gets when's they been rumbled for a rook, that look of hate hiding guilt, like as they can smother the shifty with the surly. It's the look of them as don't wear their story proud, pinned to their chest in a name like Gobfabbler, yeah? The look of them as is ashamed of it.

•

—Oh, he's a wild one, right enough, says Yapper. Whelp—that's what I calls him—Whelp, he don't half get his hackles up if a stranger come too close. First day I goes back to me crib, I had three fingers missing, bit right off. Lucky the Fixing sorts that, eh? Me crib-mates swore blind I was bonkers, but I kept at it. Lost more fingers than I has to count with, but afters a while, Whelp and me, we got to talking. Thing is though, Dog… tain't exactly made for fabbling, so getting his story were another matter.

•

But the Waiftaker General, he don't need to speak Dog to have a fair notion as to what Whelp is saying right now, on the other side of the door behind his back. And tain't nothing to do with *cats*. *Bad men* and *feed me,* maybes. Maybes even *feed me bad men*. But a lot of that barking, why, it's almost in plain English, it is, as best a mutt can articulate all em complicated consonants with its slobbery muzzle. But, well, it ain't like there's too many consonants in: *You! You! You! You!*

Yapper he smiles and carries on.

•

—Most I could get from Whelp was *river, river, river!* Which weren't getting us nowhere. Then I has an inspiration. Go ask Rake Jake Scallion, I thinks. He's a good mate to us Scruffians—well, ye'll know that on account of the grief he causes yer—and *he* weren't Fixed for the usual reasons. He don't talk about his own how and why, but maybes he'd have a notion why the Institute would be Fixing an animal of all things. So I done just that, and blow me if Jake Scallion don't know the whole story of the Scruffian dog.

• 15

So now Yapper spins his yarn, how he stopped by Rake Jake Scallion's hidey-hole in—yer don't needs to know, says he—and how Jake brung him in, give him a glass of hot gin as welcome, and listened keen as Yapper told him 'bout this mad dog he was wrangling out of rage. And after he's done, Rake Jake Scallion gazes a whiles at his latest forgery, a perfect copy of some fine Old Master's painting of David with the head of Goliath—only Goliath's face looks right familiar in a beady-eyed buzzard way. Then he nods.

•

—See, once upon a time, says Yapper, there was a spoiled little brat who'd an awful tendency to torture his pets to death. Went through a dozen mice, he did, a half dozen cats, and a good few dogs. His old man keeps bringing him new ones, but he keeps on killing em, till one day his father says enough's enough; this is the last, and if it's killed there'll be no more. Only that father happens to be the Waiftaker General, and the brat knows all about his old man's business. About the Stamp, and how's it Fixes things.

•

Old Lionel J. Reakesack, he's got his arms folded now, but the Waiftaker General, he sees a thumb come up to drift across the man's chest, like as he's minding an itch what's been scratched raw. Like when it hurts too much to scratch more, yeah, but it's still a right sore bother, so's you can't help but stroke it? And it don't exactly help none, but yer still does it anyhow, traces the pain with a gentle touch, as if to soothe it with yer thoughts, to let it know it ain't forgot.

Yapper, he just twirls his leash.

•

—So this brat has a bully idea, see. Sneaks his pet into the Institute one night, not a stickman even asking why the spiteful little turd is there, for fear of him running to his old man, getting em dismissed for imaginary insolence. He knows where the Stamp is, how to use it, how he's *going* to use it: he's only going to Fix the dog, ain't he? So's it won't ever *have* to be replaced. No matter *how* he harms it.

—Only he don't reckon on how Fixing hurts. He don't reckon on the dog going... well... barking mad.

• 16

—Now that dog don't like the little fucker to start with, and it don't trust him an inch, so when he brings the Stamp out, it does its damnedest just to get away. He has to catch it, muzzle it, tie it down while it's Fixed, and by fuck, the moment the pain starts, that dog snaps. It goes from struggling to snarling, howling and growling with all the fury it's got. Is it any bleeding wonder? It don't know what's going on, but it sure as fuck knows it ain't good. That dog was Fixed fighting for its life.

•

He feels the door shuddering at his back, does the Waiftaker General, slamming and rattling under Whelp's unending onslaught. He minds how he'd felt when his lieutenant first brung him news of this Beast of Buskerville, his wave of a hand—hardly our concern, man. But then how the sightings and stories grew and grew, till he gots to wondering whether it *were* just another rabid cur after all. If it had really been shot in the face and survived. If it were truly the fury they said it were...

But it couldn't be, he'd thought. It just couldn't be.

•

—Course, even this brainless little brat knows it ain't suitable for a pet now. Man, it near enough skins its own legs getting free of the straps as holds it down; it's all's he can do to beat it back into a cage; and once inside, well, when it manages to smash its muzzle off, there's no sodding way he's going in there to try and Scrub it. So what's the boy going to do with an immortal, indestructible beast Fixed furious at him? Except maybes order two stickmen to dump the animal in the Thames, cage and all.

•

It weren't from panic, strange as it might sound. As the Waiftaker General stood there scowling back at the Scruffian and the hawker, as they slowly moved in towards him, that were a certainty in his heart, a truth as made him hate them more for their not knowing that part of it. He were a reckless child, but it were cold anger as made him hasty in… disposing of the dog, not fear. He were like ice as he give the order, he remembers, calm as can be. But the white light of his ire did blind him, maybes.

• 17

Now the Waiftaker General he rallies himself. Bold and defiant he is as he steps forward, fists up for a fight. An old man and some *scruff*, he's thinking. He looks from one to the other, both right close now.
   —Years passed, and that boy growed up to be a man, says Yapper, inherited his father's office and all. But that was all Scallion had to tell, he said, 'cept that if I ever met him I should pass on a message.
   Only now Reakesack stands far bolder than the buzzard. Tall.
   —Sod it, says he. I'll do it myself.

•

And Reakesack punches the Waiftaker General right in the gob, spins him around in place, knocks him so hard, why, all the letters of the name *Lionel J. Reakesack* go whirling up into the air, and when they comes back down, you knows what they spell, dontcha: *Rake Jake Scallion!*
   Why, he plants his punch on that beady-eyed bugger square as the Stamp were pressed on his chest, breaking beak and busting teeth; and

the Waiftaker General, he gets the message loud and clear as it whirls him off his feet in a stagger and crumple to the floor.

•

—Scallion, he hisses, blood bubbling at his lips.

The old hawker looks a foot taller now and a fair few decades younger as he peels off the straggly beard and shnoz, sends his hat sailing off through the air with a flick of his wrist, wig and spectacles too. Why, even with the greasepaint, glue and grime as still disguises him, Rake Jake looks more beau than beggar now.

What's that, scrag? Well, of course not. Come on! Yer didn't think we'd be having an *actual* money-grubbing, child-slaving Jew in this here fabble, did yer? Not bleeding likely.

•

No, Rake Jake just knowed that him playing Fagan Shylockowitz were the best way to work the Waiftaker General: give him a hook-nose to hook his hate to, so's he don't think to sniff too deep. It ain't always a matter of fooling a mark into trusting yer, is what Jake says to Yapper, see? Sometimes it's a matter of fooling them into *dis*trusting yer… but distrusting yer the wrong way, for the wrong reason.

Tell the truth, there were likely a pinch of bitter joke to it for Jake too. The Jake *is* short for Jacob, after all.

• 18

—So we heard you was looking for Whelp, says Rake Jake Scallion. Thought we'd arrange a meeting.

—Why? says the Waiftaker General He don't say no more than that, but they can tell as he's asking about it all. Why the whole charade? Why the Scruffian should care about the dog? Why the Rake should care to help the Scruffian? Why they'd risk a Scrubbing for this savage *thing* snarling on the other side of the door? Why they'd play this game as will surely bring a terrible reckoning upon them? Why, if any harm should come to him… ?

—Why?

•

Scallion crouches down to him then, leans in close.

—If yer asking as I got the Stamp before yer time, says he, so why should I hold it against you personal like? Well, as far as I'm concerned, mate, one Waiftaker General is *all* Waiftaker Generals. But more than that? You don't get my story no more than you get his. Know this though: the only reason I'll not kill you, no matter the villainy you were begotten in, is you're as much your mother's as your father's son. And she would have loved you, I'm sure… had she lived.

• 

And now Yapper hunkers down, steadying himself with the cane.

—And if yer asking why we'd risk the wrath poured out the last time a Cuntfucker General came a cropper, he says, well, yer ought to know we has a little leverage amongst the Lords these days, peers with… peccadilloes they'd rather keep shtum. And with you to blame for the Beast and all… only reason I ain't bashing yer fucking brains in with this stick of yours is, the way I sees it, it wouldn't be right to let yer die when it's living is how most Scruffians suffer.

• 

It weren't quite then that the Waiftaker General felt fear for the first time in his life, as he realised all his stickmen didn't matter a squittery shite. It weren't as he looked into his enemies' eyes and saw not an ounce of fear in Scruffian nor Rake. It weren't as they snatched him, sudden and rough, hurled him into the centre of the room, knowing that neither was feared to finish him; for they'd both said they wasn't gonna. It were when Yapper spoke his next words, cool and quiet.

—But neither of us speaks for Whelp, says he.

• 19

The bloodcurdling howl that rang out across Old Nichol Rookery then, when Yapper and Jake opened the door to let the Beast of Buskerville meet its maker… the terrible sound that chilled to the bone everyone as heard it, woke babes as was sleeping and made it as they'd not sleep for two days after, the sound as give even grown men screaming nightmares for weeks… well, only Yapper and Jake knows for sure which of the two that horrible sound come from, and they ain't saying. Ask em and they just smiles a little smile of mischief, sneaky fuckers.

•

—Maybes it come from the monster, Yapper'll say, from that dread fiend as still stalks the backstreets and alleys of Old London Town to this very day, that vicious brute as any man in his right mind would surely put down for the mad dog as he is. Or then again, maybes it come from old Whelp.

—We was already halfways out the door, Jake'll say. Giving Whelp some space to play a little with his new chew toy. Giving him some time to… renew his acquaintance with his old master, savvy?

—All's the time in the world, Yapper'll say.

•

Yeah, that's right, scrag, you heard right. Three whole—

What? Dunno. *Nobody* knows how Whelp kept him alive that long. Maybes the dog brung him dead rats or summat, but I ain't sure how that could work; don't rightly know why the Waiftaker General wouldn't leg it if Whelp even left the room. Yapper has some crazy idea as Whelp bit off his own—cause it would've grown back—but that seems *bonkers!* No, it's a mystery. Ain't nobody even knows *why* Whelp kept him alive for that matter. Maybes he were thinking like Yapper, that killing were too quick.

•

All's we know is Whelp played guard-dog to his prisoner, kept him caged in mortal terror—and no small amount of pain most likely—till one day… one day…

He let him go.

Yep, just like that. He just upped and went offsky, out the door and away, leaving the Waiftaker General to cower in his own filth till he got up the courage to crawl out of the room, and down the stairs, and out into the night.

Although there's some as say not all of him got let go, right enough, that old Whelp kept a few… souvenirs.

• 20

Oh, yeah, there's some as say that the Waiftaker General, he's short a few fingers now under his fancy kidskin gloves, or that his lanky-limbed stride is… a little ungainly and lolloping now cause half his toes ain't on his feet no more. Or on account of him being one bollock shy of a pair, perhaps.

Ain't nobody knows but the Waiftaker General and the Beast of Buskerville himself what that dog done to him in all the time he was prisoner. And it seems to me as ain't neither of em really gots the words to tell that fabble.

•

This much we does know though. When he finally staggered out of Old Nichol, that night, so they says, every hair on the Waiftaker General's head were white as the driven snow, from the fear that dog had struck in him. And whatever the scars he might have in places as can't be seen, that there hair ain't the only sign of it. Maybes he's hiding something more, as they says, like as a Stamp can be hid by a buttoned-up shirt. But yer can *see* the fear as in a nipper's flinch at a raised fist.

Fixed in him.

•

Maybes some madness too, I reckons. See, it weren't the hideous stumbling state of him as made the passers-by recoil in horror as he staggered and crawled the long way back, by a route as didn't really need to be a tenth as long, to the Institute. No, it werent even all the blood and shit filthing his mauled, naked form as made them shove him away when he tried to grab em by the lapels. It were the ungodly yowling as he clawed and pawed at em.

Cause he weren't talking the Queen's English now, but the Beast's Dog.

•

It would be peachy to think that were the end of the Waiftaker General for good, right then and there, but sadly it ain't so, scrags. Stories like his ain't ended so easy. No, he went offsky for a good long while, but… well, he's had a whole lot of years to mend his mind since then. And he ain't mended his ways *at all*, the fucker.

Still, you mind how old Whelp, he put a fear in him as'll *never* mend, and if yer ever has a run-in with that fucker…

You just gives him a little growl, hear?

# The Taking of the Stamp

## PART ONE

### • 1

Alright, me nippy little scamps and scrags, me gangle-limbed scallywags, scofflaws too. All of yer, shusht! Shut yer gobs and park yer arses, pin yer ears back and hark at me fabble. Don't gimme yer *heard it*. Don't gimme yer *lived it*. We gots us two strays set to take the Stamp, so yer knows the score, knows how it goes. As sure as me name's Gobfabbler Halyard-Dunkling, Esquire—and a *bugger-yer-mum* to any what says it ain't—it's time to tattle the fabble we tells all newbs, the fabble of The Taking of the Stamp.

•

Now, yer has to imagine the clock rolled back, yer city with its skyscrapers scrubbed, no pickly Gerkin, no pointy Shard, no Eye whirling groanhuffs up to the sky. Nope, this were the old days of rookery slums, steam trains and sewer stink, pea-souper smogs, of horseflap splattering cobbled streets what nippers in tackety boots run clomping on with hoop and stick. This were the bad old days, when Ripper Vicky still stalked Whitechapel, just a harmless old hag them tarts would think, till *slash! slice!* and their livers was food, and off she'd slink back to Buck House!

•

And this were the bad old days when Ripper Vicky weren't even the worst, for sure as yer Empress of India were guilty of all's her arselicking bootboys fingered them Hindoo Thugs for in the foreign lands she'd her eye on, why, here in the Heart of Empire, she'd her Waiftaker General and his stickmen to rip us too, to rip yer from yer mam's arms in some raid, fibbing as she'd stole yer—not a fine fib fabbled for the fun, no, a fucker's *lie* painting Jews as Christ-killers, babysnatchers, like, to paint their own sins as salvation.

• 

Back in them bad old days, twas the groanhuffs had the Stamp, see? Weren't a workhouse waif as was safe from being sold to the scrufftraders, nor a street Arab as didn't live in fear of being scrobbled, chucked in the back of a Grey Mary. Off to the Institute ye'd go then, where they'd put the Stamp on yer, and oh, how ye'd scream as they Fixed yer forever, sob as they sold yer for a Scruffian, to sweep the chimneys or clean the mills.

This here's a fabble of them bad old days.

How we brung em down.

• 2

Look at that door behind yer, eh? Yeah, you too, Joey. Quit yer scofflaw scoffing. I knows *you were there*, and *it ain't like it's told*, but bollocks to yer *historical accuracy*. I likes the airship, so shut it. For once. All of yer, listen. You most of all, you strays as has made yer choice. If yer wants to join us, yer has to know what it means to be a Scruffian. So picture a crib like this, all the liberated Scruffians in it gathered round their fabbler, yeah, just like us here. Now, look at that door…

BOOM!

• 

Picture that door come flying in! Smashed from its hinges and splintering frame! Like a tombstone toppled, down it comes—DOOM!—a scrag underneath it yelping, crushed! And there in the doorway—buggering shite!—it's stickmen, me scruffs, the Waiftaker's men, a mob of the brutes, all bowlers and billy clubs, piling in. *Run! Run!* the shout goes up. The scrags they scatter! The scamps they scarper—this way and that, dodging clubs, ducking legs. But outside the room, it ain't no better—*Stickmen! Everywhere! Save yer skins!*

But battering rams crash through boarded windows. Ain't nowheres to run. Nowheres.

•

So it's *Fight!* now, *Fight!* and *Scruffians, STAMP!* Why, the scallywags and scofflaws, they's already at it, sharp as that door went, diving and rolling to chains and coshes, coming up on one knee with a knife in this hand or a spikestick in that, to spring, to pounce on the first stickmen in. They're smashing teeth with iron links, and slashing throats with cold steel, skewering guts and gullets, goolies too.

But the stickmen keeps coming, keeps pouring in, their clubs cracking skulls, smacking scallywags down, bashing scofflaw brains into the dust! No mercy, no quarter, it's bloody murder.

•

They fight, them Scruffians. Still they fight. Knock one nipper down, another scrabbles to her feet again, crunching broke bones straight again, wiping blood from wounds already healed, springing back to how's they're Fixed. Leaping back into the fray. Being Fixed makes for a handy slave—*resilient*—but once they's free…

Still, the billy clubs swing, and brains splatter walls. And if even a smashed conk mends *relatively* sharpish, well, yer ain't got the wits to do sod all in the meantime. So one by one, them fiesty Scruffians is beaten down until's there's only one, alone against the mob.

• 3

That last scruff standing weren't even no scofflaw like Joey, nor even a scallywag, just a scrag no bigger than Puckerscruff there. And how come's I knows it? Cause it *were* our Puckerscruff. Yeah! Puckerscruff, he'd be kinda the princess in this fabble, see—kinda a princess in real life too, if yer catches me drift—oh, don't huff, Puck, yer knows it's true. Anyways, it were our very own urchin, armed with just his spikes—and only half of what he has now from all's his Stamp-tweaking—Puckerscruff, dukes up, back to the wall!

—Come ahead, says he.

•

Fiesty little fucker, for all his flounce. Little hole of freedom in his Stamp—show em, Puck—where's he snuck his lucky penny in, botched the Fixing. Rough trading even afore he was Scruffian too, thruppence for a thump for any as paid. So Puckerscruff, he's holding em off with just the gleam of his knuckles.

But oh, from the doorway then comes a ripple in that mob. They parts from the back like the Red Sea, and striding through comes a fiend, a beady-eyed, beak-nosed blackguard, white hair slicked back like a skull-cap… the Waiftaker General himself.

• 

Frockcoat and cane, a fancy dan fucker, he fixes our scrag in his icy gaze.

—You have my property in your possession, *scruff*, he spits.

—What's that? says Puckerscruff. Me liberty? Me life?

And he gives a growl at the man as makes him flinch. The Waiftaker General gathers himself though.

—You know whereof I speak, says he.

—No idea, says the scrag, though he knowed fine well, for he'd the most precious prize—

Flashjack! Fucking… *yeah*, it's the plans, but *they* ain't s'posed to know that yet! Shhh!

For he'd a precious prize… a prize as might change *everything*.

•

So, slam! Puckerscruff, he kicks his foot into the floor, and the floorboard goes down beneath his foot, flying up at the other end, smack in the Waiftaker General's knackers—or knacker, if the rumours was true—bending him double, so's that saucy little scrag can leapfrog right over him. The stickmen's still parted, see, from letting His Nibs through, a clear path to the door, which Puckerscruff darts now, befores they can even move to grab him. Oh, but what an uproar as he slides under the grasp of the brutes at the doorway, out into the hall.

• 4

Out in the hallway, there ain't no escape though, stickmen at the front door, coming out of rooms to left and right, hauling scamps and scrags by poles with nooses on the end, dragging scallywags with skulls like dropped watermelons by their feet, leaving streaks of blood and brain on floorboards, dumping the twitchy wrecks in a pile at the front door, for collection. For Scrubbing. That's how it were back then. No mercy for Scruffians as has slipped their chains, run offsky from their master. Just coshes and nooses, and a bloody scouring of yer Stamp, of yer *everything*.

•

It's a horror of a sight, it is, but it's a sight seen in an instant, for the Waiftaker General's already bellowing: *Get him!* and the stickmen are already turning, clocking the scrag. They're behind him, ahead of him, every which way. Every way but the chance he snatches, up onto a table, leaping for a banister, scrambling up and over to the stairs of the big house what this gang's took for a crib. Up those stairs he legs it, fast as his pins can carry him, stickmen at his heels, taking two steps for his one, hands clamping—

•

CRASH! CRACKARACKACRASH BOOM FUCKING WALLOP! Why, Puckerscruff's near dragged down himself by the meaty paw on his shoulder, but the stickman's grip slips as them rotten stairs give out beneath him and down he goes, down they all goes, all but Puckerscruff, nimble as a monkey, whirling to catch a handhold and swing and scrabble to safety. Phew! But he don't even have time to relish the shrieks of stickmen spiked on broken wood or with bones sticking from their tin flutes. There's the Waiftaker General below, spitting orders, snarling rage, so it's up and offsky. Shift it, Puckerscruff! Move!

•

But where to? he thinks as he hits the landing. There's corridors, rooms, but he don't know the escapes. Ain't his crib, see? Just a safe house for tonight on his way through the city, on his mission. And oh, but he curses hisself for what he's brung down on them as took him in. He's Scrubbed em all, he has.

He runs down a hallway dark as his thoughts, hears stickmen on the other stairs though. Bollocks! Into a room... of boarded windows! *Bollocks!* And ain't nuffink else but a wardrobe...

In he dives, pulling the door shut after.

He pants. He puffs. He catches his breath.

So there's he is in the darkness, Puckerscruff, hunkered down to a ball, peering out through the crack where the door's ajar. Only… slowly he gets this queer niggly feeling as he ain't alone. To be specifical, he gets the feeling of hot air on his neck, of panting as ain't his. And the stink of bad breath what goes with it. So, slowly he turns to see, there in the dark, the white of a dog's teeth, and the whites of a Scruffian's eyes behind it—Whelp and Yapper, by crikey.

•

Only ever been one Scruffian dog, and that's Whelp. Only ever been one scamp could handle him, and that's Yapper. Both of them's hid in there already, and Whelp… ain't happy to have company.

He's set for snarling, is Whelp, smelling the Waiftaker General on Puckerscruff's hands. Whelp and that fucker got history, see, that madman being the fiend as Fixed a poor pup, that mutt being the beast what turned the bastard's hair white—but that's another fabble. Point is, Whelp's lips curl, and he give a growl—only cuts it off as Yapper quiets him sharpish.

Puckerscruff… thinks.

•

Now. Ain't a word passes between em, they can't make a peep, so all's Yapper can do is cock his head curious like Whelp's as Puckerscruff undoes the collar round his neck—yeah, even back then, scamp—buckles it round the dog's. Queer, thinks Yapper. If that ain't flummox enough, *then* the scrag lifts his hands up like Whelp's pointy ears, then dances em like horse's hooves going clip-clop, does it over, all's while mouthing… well, summat.

That's right, mate: *Foxtrot.* Yer sharp for a stray. Pity Yapper weren't, for he just gawps like this poor bugger's gone bonkers.

•

So Yapper he ain't got a clue what's what. All's he knows is Puckerscruff's a molly urchin what rapped on the crib door whiles the gaslighter were doing his evening rounds, begging hospitality—as any Scruffian would be an arsewipe to refuse. And there was murmerings with the boss, summat about an Order of Chaeronea—which one scallywag told him's a not-so-secret society of molly punters. So, Yapper's busy trying to make sense of it all, when Puckerscruff puts the cherry on top.

A finger to his lips, he tips a wink, and slips out of the wardrobe.

• 6

Yapper don't know what to do then, so he just waits, huddled down behind Whelp, keeping him schtum with *there, there* and *easy oasy, boy,* but in Dog, natch, which Yapper speaks fluent... well, I says *speak,* but *there, there* and *easy oasy, boy* is atcherly silent in Dog, says Yapper, which is where's most humans bollocks it up. Anyways, they waits through the kerfuffle and cries. They waits through the *nab him*'s and *grab him*'s. They waits through the thumps and thuds, the mumbles and rumbles. They waits till the whole house falls silent. Then they waits some more.

•

Finally, Yapper creaks the wardrobe door open for a peek. Nuffink. He points Whelp to pad out, soft 'cept for claws scratching floorboards, and out he tiptoes afters. A whistle holding Whelp at his heel, he peeps from the room. Still nuffink. So down he goes, into the horror of an happy crib stripped bare but for splatters and smears. He wanders that room what we started in, gives a little whine as makes Whelp nuzzle his hand. At last, he swallers a sob, and it's offsky, to the sneakhole of a cellar window—safe way out, he reckons.

Wrongly.

•

He wrangles Whelp up the crates afore him, shoves the dog's wriggly arse out the window, squiggling himself afters, through the broken bars. Even as he thrashes from the bushes though—what's this? Whelp growling ahead. And out of the shrubbery he scrambles to see an eyepatched brigand in tatty overcoat and battered topper—a scrufftrader! vulturing the raid for scraps such as this. His pistol points at a snarling, slouch-sprung Whelp.

—Good doggy, he sneers, and BANG!

Yowl, howl, scream—oh, the racket as Yapper made then. He were pouncing himself even as the pistol swung, and…

BANG!

•

It's all a jumble then, as Yapper fabbles it, what with a bullet in his brain whiles the Stamp's slowly bouncing him back to how's he were Fixed. He *fancies* he were in a rattly cart when the slug popped from his noggin, but in truth, the next he remembers clear is being brung out into blinding light, dumped on grass.

—Yer scruff, says the scrufftrader.

A lad's face peers down at Yapper then—but white as Death, eyebrows painted on black, black teardrops on his cheeks.

—Uncle… he says. It… ain't right.

And that's how Yapper met Joey Picaroni.

• 7

Now showfolk is good folks, let's be clear, but *clowns*… Yer see them horror flicks about evil clowns? *Evil clowns?* Why, if that ain't as breath-wasting as *arrogant toffs*. You ask Joey there how jolly his uncle were, how his belt beat Joey into Pierrot's tears since he were a nipper. Cause oh, how the groanhuffs chortled to see this pititful pint-size slapsticked to sobbing!

But Joey were growed to lanky now, see, so his red-nosed, blood-grinned wicked uncle needs a new moppet for the show. And think of the pratfalls as a Scruffian can suffer!

•

Whassat? No, Joey weren't a Scruffian then, weren't really Joey Picaroni. But that's the name he took, so that's the only name as we'll call him, savvy?

Anyways, next Yapper knows he's heaved up by Joey, carted off through caravans and cages, to a tent, where's the boss clown has Joey lash Yapper hand and foot, pound tent pegs in the soil. Gives Joey a backhand slap for backchat too—why, for a tick Yapper fancies the lad might take that mallet to his uncle. But, no. It's a sad Pierrot as leaves Yapper staked, all alone now, all alone.

•

They says it's darker afore the dawn. Well, this *were* dawn and the darkest Yapper ever knowed. His every crib-mate snatched for Scrubbing, sold to the circus hisself, even his best chum Whelp left in brain-splattered shrubbery, left to rouse alone and *rowowowl* for a lost pack... it's near too much to bear for Yapper, even when's that Pierrot sneaks him a crust of bread, round noon.

—I knows scruffs don't need it, mumbles the lad. But still...

Afternoon, evening, there ain't a hope left in Yapper, he's *disconsolatrated*, when—wait! Through his sniffles he hears...

A *snuffle!*

•

And then it's Whelp! Wriggling in under the tent flap, lolloping to him, to slobber his face, clamber over him wagtailed, and oh, how it soars his spirits, and how he oughta have *knowed* Whelp'd sniff him out. In a trice then, he's got Whelp gnawing at his ropes... he's loose! Now, time to be offsky, toot sweet, eh? So outs they sneak—

—into a circus funfair in full oompah, Yapper and Whelp back behind the sideshows and stalls, true, but a hustle here too of acrobat, liontamer, strongman, juggler... *clown!*

Yapper ducks beneath a caravan.

The clown feet pass.

• 8

Now, it's a curious thing as Yapper finds when he crawls toward the back of the caravan, aiming for the camp's edge and away, for Whelp he sits on his arse, won't budge. *Come on*, says Yapper, and *Whatcha doing?* and other such things, but Dog ain't good for explifications, so he starts crawling back; and that's when Whelp shifts... in the wrong direction altogether. Why, they *could* be escaping, but no, Whelp's offsky for the carnival, and what's Yapper to do? He yips, *Come back!* and yaps it bossier, but he's no choice but follow... to the midway itself.

•

Freak show, geek show, wrestlers, boxers, horsie carousel and hook-a-duck, it were a wondrous whirlymajig... for all's but Yapper, whose only wonder is the mad mutt leading him by bally cloths and barkers, plonking his arse down now before, of all things...

—Kaarlo Cjaselneski! booms this walrus-moustached magician on a stage. Greatest escapologeest of ze 'ole vorld! All ze vay frum Greater Ünkel, Wülgaria! Zeese show ees... ees...

All flustery to heave Whelp away by his new collar, it takes Yapper a second to see how the magician's gawping at him, glancing sidewise, shifty.

—Cancelled! booms Kaarlo.

•

And Kaarlo's into the crowd, quick as a flash, and first it's Yapper's own hand on Whelp's collar dragging him with the dog, then it's the magician's hand on Yapper's, hauling him through the air, on stage, the scamp squirming bitey, flailing all the way through the curtains and even as he's planted on a seat in the waggon, snarling fierce as Whelp learned him, until the very instant Kaarlo rips the moustache from his mug and...

—Jake! says Yapper.

For Kaarlo Cjaselneski were none other than Rake Jake Scallion, rakiest Rake as ever was, and friend to every Scruffian.

•

But Jake, he ain't fussed with Yapper, no, he's down at Whelp's collar, unbuckling it, babbling *Glory be! A miracle!* And he's rattling his forger's eyeglass and tools from a drawer, and afore yer know it, half the collar's studs are off, and...

—Gotcha! says he.

For there in his tweezers is the teeniest scrap, yellowy this side, dark the other, Puckerscruff's prize, a microphotograph what he'd got from the Order of Chaeronea—from Oscar Wilde hisself, they says—who got it from beds and blackmail: plans of the Institute itself; of the very vault where's the Stamp were kept.

• 9

Yeah, honest! Oscar Wilde! So they *says*, anyways. I hears we offered him the Stamp for it, afore he were sent down. He were tempted. Says he didn't want to be no Dorian though. More's the pity. He'd have made a right good Rake, Oscar—

A Rake? Them's the few and far between folks as were Fixed as adults. Like Jake Scallion, savvy? Ain't many, as it weren't thought wise, harder to smack down.

Nah, some of them nobs *might* have fancied immortality, but they reckoned the soul writ in yer Stamp weren't *real*. That yer weren't human no more.

•

nyways, so Yapper learns what Jake's heard, about Puckerscruff's mission, how he were to fetch the plans back to the nearest thing as Scruffians have to a boss of bosses, Foxtrot.

—*Oooooh*, says Yapper finally twigging what Puckerscruff were miming in the wardrobe.

It's up to them now, Jake tells him. They gotta be offsky, get them plans to where they belong.

—And you better do it quick, says a voice.

And there stands Joey Picaroni, at that curtain where's the waggon's side is dropped as stage.

—One scrufftrader and a dozen stickmen, says he. And they're looking for you.

•

The stickmen are here! Now all's a flurry! Jake rummages through this trunk and that, through guises all labeled to his fancy, with the letters of his name guddled up: a Polish intellectual, Aaron Laski-Lekjce; a Swedish matchgirl, Rosalie-Jean Klack; a German watchmaker, Alaric Jake Sonkel; a Scottish industrialist, Josiah Leacklanker—

—There's an extra aitch in that, says Joey.

—All the aitches dropped round here, says Jake, can't let them *all* go to waste.

At last he settles on Eleasar Jinkalock, a miserly muckamuck, English as tuppence, with rusty chains for Yapper and Whelp to finish the look.

•

Then Joey gives em directions for sneaking out, and where's he'll *rondy-views* em.

—I'll cause a distraction, says he, and off he pops.

And that's how Joey Picaroni come to run away from the circus, join the Scruffians without being Fixed yet… making him the first ever stray, I s'pose. For he'd had it with his uncle's beatings, he were sickened by the world, and he were out to strike a blow against it.

It's also how Joey come to burn that boss clown's caravan to ash, scrufftrader, stickmen and his uncle inside.

Which were a good distraction, right enough.

## PART TWO

### • 1

There was four of them then set out from Stepney Green—which is where they was—weaving their way south west. There were Eleasar Jinkalock, the fusty fop, in the dandiest gent's most tattered togs. Behind were his manservant, face stripped of greasepaint for the first time in forever—

Well, it *was* in this fabble, Joey.

Cause I says so.

Afore him meanwhiles, on their chains, was Whelp and Yapper—which weren't as queer a sight as yer might fancy. No, Scruffians were out there to be seen, alright; the Trade just weren't to be discussed, weren't *acknowledged*. Weren't *delicate*.

•

Yeah, you hear of some nob with a pet monkey back in them days, like as not that's code for Scruffian. A monkey in a toff's portrait, or a midget in a king's: Scruffian. A *miser's housepet*—that's how they used to put it, on account of a Scruffian don't need fed, on account of a Scruffian being Fixed. Don't get sick much neither, unless yer blade slips while's yer tweaking yer Stamp. So, yeah, there was just a few cocked snoots from passers-by, and the best as can be said is *some* were at the master's cold heart.

•

So, it's Cable Street they makes for, on a secret mission to bring the most precious prize as had ever been swiped to Foxtrot Wainscot Hottentot III.

Foxy here's sorta the boss of bosses, see—*sorta*—ever since Nuffinmuch O'Anyfink gone offsky, which were so far back ain't many more'n Foxy minds it. The time of *pirates*, like. Nuff were king—of the tinkers too, by way of his da as was killed when he were scrobbled. But Nuff were too Scruffian for such bollocks, so one day he just lit out for elsewheres leaving Foxtrot to run the show.

•

Not that Foxy's much for playing Lord Muck neither, says it's more of a *fixer* thing, really, a *facilliotator*. Like Nuff were a hero cause he figgered out Stamp-tweaking, Foxy's the boss cause… well, he's *foxy*. Course, it made him a wanted man back then. The Waiftaker General didn't even have his name, but he knowed there was *someone* masterminding all the Grey Mary ambushes and liberations. So Foxy, he lives on the lam, flitting crib to crib, hid so sneakily there's only one scrag as might know his whereabouts.

And that's what brung em to Squirlet's opium den.

• 2

In an alley off Cable Street, it were, among boozers and brothels, between a slop-shop and a gin-shop, down steps worn treacherous, just one big room, lamplit low as the rafters, all smogged with the puffing of sailors and such curled up on higgledy-piggledy bunks. Soon as they's in the door, a scamp runs up to em—Vermintrude Toerag by name. Filthy as sin and snottery to boot, but that don't stop Jake from gathering her up into a best mates' hug… as makes Joey's nose wrinkle when she comes in whiffing distance.

—Where's Squirlet? says Jake.

•

So Vermintrude leads em a zigzag through the bunks, Yapper dumping his chain now's they're safe, taking Whelp's off too. Up some creaky wooden stairs they goes, into Squirlet's crib, into a babble of Scruffians, a maze of oriental screens, to a nook where Squirlet Nicely's just dismissing some smuggler from a consultation. Ain't nobody can't hide nuffink like Squirlet can, see?

She narrows her eyes at Puckerscruff's collar on Whelp, purses her lips. Jake don't even need to tell her what's what.

—Amateurs, she tuts. This way.

And she whirls to the panelling behind her, pokes a knothole.

*Click.*

•

Down the secret passage Joey follows Yapper and Whelp, who follows Jake and Trude, who follows Squirlet. Joey ain't wholly sure he's invited, he's just worrying as they's mistook him for Scruffian, indeed, when there's a merry cry—*Jake! Whelp! Yapper!*—as flows into *What the fuck's this fucker doing here?* and a knife at his throat, a scallywag with fiery hair.

—This cuntfucker ain't Scruffian, hisses Flashjack Scarlequin.

—Easy there, says Jake. He's sound.

—Oh? says Flashjack.

And just like that, his arm's round Joey's shoulder, and Flashjack's firing up his footlong pipe with a fingersnap.

—Well, welcome, matey!

•

Now Joey, he ain't never seen a hellion trick like Flashjack's sparking flame from his thumb, so that don't exactly settle him none. And it don't help that this sparky scallywag's no sooner playing best chum than he's off again, whirling down—*What the what?!*—to the collar round Whelp's neck, looking up with horror on his mug, at Jake, at Yapper.

—Puckerscruff? Me peachy Puck? What's happened? What they done to him? Why's Whelp—?

—Jack! pipes a voice.

And from the shadows of the hidey what the passage opens into, out steps a scamp in moustache and monocle.

Foxtrot.

• 3

—So Puckerscruff's scrobbled, says Foxtrot once they's all sat round the table in his den, an attic stashroom at the top of *another* secret passage from the hidey.

—He can't be Scrubbed, says Flashjack. I'd *know* if he were Scrubbed.

Him and Puckerscruff were sweethearts, see. If this were some groan-huff story, it'd be Flashjack for hero, rescuing the dainty damsel, but this fabble's for you strays to savvy the Scruffian life, where's *all* in that war room, *all* of em's heroes. Still, Flashjack he's for storming the Institute pronto, on his ownsome if need be.

—What if… ? he whimpers.

•

—The Waiftaker General won't Scrub him, old chap, says Foxtrot. He's too valuable. But… what would Puck himself say was the priority here, Jack?

And as Whelp lays his head on the scallywag's knee to comfort him, Flashjack hangs his own, and in a quivery voice:

—The Stamp, says he.

For he knows whatever his sweetheart's suffering now, it were all risked bravely for that precious prize, for them pinhead plans what Foxtrot's tweezering even now into a stanhoscope—which he screws to a magic lantern, with a nod for Flashjack to fire it up as he dims the lamp.

•

And there on a dirty linen sheet nailed between two posts, why, it's the plans of the Institute's nine floors, from basement cells to the Fixing Room itself, and the vault at the heart of it. It's wondrous intricate, even a little legend at the bottom as puffs the magical miniaturisation: Dancer's Daguerrotypical Diminution, it says, as Joey tells a stymied Yapper what tugs his sleeve while's Foxtrot and Squirlet discurses and deliberates.

—*Daggery typical*, whispers Yapper, eyes wide. Can you reads anyfink? Even all's of Mister Dickens?

—I'm less of a Copperfield, more of a Kropotkin man, says Joey.

•

Meanwhiles, Joey's own curiosity's niggling. For a bit he just watches Foxtrot figgering routes through the Institute with Eleasar Jinkalock's cane, but finally he just has to blurt it.

—*Why?* he whispers to Yapper. Why the *moustache?*

—It's a disguise, says Yapper. Silly.

—But… he's… for the love of… that's *ridiculous.*

—Is it? says Yapper. What'll *you* mind of his face when yer leaves here?

Poor Joey Picaroni's still trying to answer that one when *It's settled then!* says the moustacheoed mite himself. And turns to peer at Joey.

—Old chap, says he, I understand you consider yourself… an ally.

48

So before long Foxtrot's laying out his plan, not the full-on frontal assault as Flashjack's riled for, nor the sneaky night-time catburglarising Squirlet fancies, but an infiltration, disguises and all. Squirlet, Flashjack, Trude and… Joey?

—And me, declares Yapper even as the stray give his nod.

Foxtrot, he looks at the scamp as has lost every crib-mate, and he ain't one to argue. Besides, they's like to need every scruff if they's to steal the Stamp.

—And rescue Puckerscruff, says Flashjack.

—That too, says Foxy.

And he turns to Vermintrude.

—Spruce up, says he. The footlights call.

•

A right little actress is Vermintrude, see. Stinky as a sewer rat's arsehole if she ain't on, but wipe her down, dress her up, and send her into a plodhouse to loose the waterworks as a poor lost daughter of the hoity toity, she'll have em eating from the palm of the hand she picks her nose with. There weren't much missed back then from Earwigger working the shoeshine network, or Lightfinger Larker going after deeds and documents instead of wallets and wipes, but when yer needed a shufty round a rozzer's records, that were Trudy's speciality.

•

Half an hour later then, why, here's Flashjack sauntering out the opium den's door, skipping up the steps, and offsky down the lane. Then out comes Eleasor Jinkalock, with his mangy mutts, canine and kiddiwink, and his manservant at his back as before, but with two ever so adorable tykes added to the retinue, Squirlet and Vermintrude—all spick and span—why, it's his two nieces looking pitifully pretty as a picture in their mourning gowns and bonnets—oh, the poor things as must've lost their ma and da and been taken in by this 'orrible miser of an uncle.

•

Down the alley they goes, to where Flashjack's on the driver's bench of a landau what he's *whoa*'ing to an halt amid the bustle of Cable Street—

not far from where's we helped block them blackshirts… now *that's* a fabble. That were afters though, when—

Alright, alright.

So, in goes Mister Jinkalock, and Yapper to his side, Whelp to his feet, and them two nieces sat facing, while's Joey, he clambers his way up to the groom's seat, looking right nervy in that precarious perch.

—I'll try not to bounce yer arse too much, Flashjack grins back.

And they's off.

• 5

They heads out into the kerfuffle of Cable Street, turns north up Leman. Through Shoreditch they goes, to the City Road, and round onto Pentonville, rattling over the cobbles when's the traffic ain't so bad, but mostly going not much faster than yer'd go in rush hour these days. They's almost at King's Cross and St Pancras, when Flashjack give a little whistle, takes the pipe from his gob with one hand and swivels it to point the stem forwards as he slows the horses.

Jake peers past him. Up ahead, three peelers is stopping coaches and carts, searching em.

•

Jake tips a nod to Squirlet and she ganders over her shoulder—Arse!

—Yapper, down, she says. Whelp, shift.

And she's off her seat, shoving Whelp aside, ignoring his growl, to tweak this and twiddle that, and hey presto! a panel goes sliding back of Jake's legs. Trust Squirlet to have a smuggler's hidey in her carriage, eh? So in goes Yapper and in goes Whelp. Takes a bit of coaxing, truth be told, and a near loss of Squirlet's nose, but eventually Yapper persuades the dog.

So, as they reaches the peelers, ain't hide nor hair of em fugitives.

•

But life ain't so easy as when the jackboots kicks yer door in, or stops yer car in a posh neighbourhood on account of yer colour, that yer can just smile, wave yer hand and say, These ain't the Scruffians yer looking for. No, maybe it's the *Wotcher, guv'nor* as Flashjack give the sergeant, or maybe it's Squirlet's glare at the peeler as has her lift her veil, but them peelers smells Scruffians. And even as Jake puts on the pomp, one peeler kicks a panel as sounds hollow. As sounds a growl.

—Oh well, says Flashjack.

But he's grinning.

•

And the bit of his pipe stays clamped in teeth, but the stem whirls in his hand—why, it ain't nowt but a twelve-inch spike with a tip as gleams cold steel… until it's in and out the back of one peeler's neck, smeared blood-red now, and darting again, right into the next peeler's eye, deep! The sergeant, he stands there gawping. He fumbles for his whistle, even gets it to his gob as Flashjack somersaults, lands on one knee at the man's feet. Drives that spike up under his chin.

Catches the whistle as the bodies fall.

• 6

They takes the cobbles now hell for leather, weaving the traffic of the road in a carriage as weren't built for darting, nor for the tight streets they turn up, smashing stalls and scattering folks to doorways, Joey Picaroni clinging on for dear life in the groom's seat, his noggin near lopped when Flashjack takes em through an arch as low as it's narrow. No helicopters nor radios for the plods in em days though, so *eventually*, as they reaches Camden Town, Flashjack lets the horses slow to a steady trot. They's in the clear. And Hampstead Heath ain't far.

•

So they rides up high on the Heath, by a trail as leads em to the tinker camp they's headed for—

No, these weren't Romani; they was Scotch… Summer Walkers, *tinsmiths*.

Tinkers and Scruffians has always been tight, see. Plenty of us come from em, taken by the stickmen, like Nuff. And they gets the same tone in *tinker* what we gets in *scruff*. So we scratches each other's backs. Like, as them scruffs ride into the camp of carts and bow tents, how Flashjack tosses the peeler's whistle to one.

—Bit of tin any use to yer? he says.

•

Yeah, there's even the fabbles of Tinker Bill, who'll knock on the tradesman's door of some townhouse, asking, *Mend yer pots, ma'am?* And there'll be some Scruffian chained, fancying no more of Bill than the other groanhuffs as does nuffink for her. But what's this? Bill's dropped summat! And, *Ain't I a butterfingers!* says he as he kneels by the scamp, slips her a skellington key, and whispers she'll know when's to run. And blow me, but not long afters, there's some almighty havoc at the front door. And that's yer scamp's chance to slip her shackles and be offsky.

• 

But most of all's, any Scruffian as has had their Stamp tweaked… if it weren't done by a tinker's hand, it were done by a tinker's wits. It's one thing an accident in the mills as cuts wildness into some scallywag's chest; it's another to finick out the fear whacked deep into a workhouse scamp. Or to gives yerself horns like as an hellion might. If it weren't for Nuff bringing us together, most liberated Scruffians would like as not have an arse on their elbow, savvy? That were why our heroes were come, for a tweaking of *hextrardinary* complexification.

• 7

Peeling white knuckles from his perch then, Joey come down into the hullaballoo of hugs and handshakes, and afters stew at the campfire and chatter as swings from merry to maudlin, he watches curious as they gets down to business. All but Flashjack—cause who'd know where's to begin with a Stamp so chopped yer wonders how's he ain't got bleeding tentacles!—they all strips to their waists, and the tinkers set to tweaking. Joey he's flummoxed at the nipples as appear on Yapper's back… till the scalpel's put to peeling the patch… and the needle and thread come out.

•

Rake Jake Scallion don't get done neither, right enough. He don't get a Stampless chest growed on his back, sliced off, and stitched to his front so's when they's finished, with the stitches hid, all em Scruffians could pass for littl'uns as ain't never even seen the inside of the Institute.

No, Jake's busy at his own part, sat on a rock by the fire with a tin tray on his lap for table, eyeglass in and quill in hand, or notary's stamp, to forge the indenture papers, signed and sealed, as says them waifs was bought fair and square.

•

—Here, says one tinker lad of a size with Flashjack and Joey. Youse two'll be needing summat tattier to wear.

So offsky they trots, to a tent, while's Squirlet and Vermintrude follows some girls, to change into garments as weren't never more aptly called threads.

As he pulls his new breeches up and knots a string for a belt, Joey clocks that Stamp of Flashjack's—show em, Jack.

Yer ain't wrong, mate. He can't even mind where all em tweaks began—can yer, Jack?

Anyways, that's why Flashjack were left as is. Fuck knows, another tweak and he might explode.

•

There were some *heated debate*, as they says, over Whelp then. Yapper, he says the dog's Stamp, well, it's mostly hid by his fur, see, and even where it *does* show all's they need do is muck him up, and if Whelp can't come *into* the Institute with em, well he can drop em off with Jake, be there's for backup. But Squirlet, she ain't having none of it. The stickmen's looking for a scruff with a dog, says she. And a lolloping scallywag dog like Whelp's distinctive. No, she says, *no*, and Foxy put her in charge. Nuff said.

• 8

So now here they is, five workhouse waifs straight out of their stripy shirts and shifts, and back in the clothes as they came in with, each with their own certificate of sale now, one guinea per gamin, and three pounds six shillings each for the beansprouts, all made out to Eleasor Jinkalock from Whitechapel and Spitalfields Union Workhouse on Whitechapel High Street—

No, it weren't the Charles Street one, Jack.

*No, it weren't.* That were the infirmary by then, where they brung Ripper Vicky's dead.

And you wasn't even there, Puckerscruff, so keep yer oar out.

Says yer arse!

•

These orphans, so the cover story went, was to serve in Mister Jinkalock's Most Illuminating Demonstration, to the board of the Central London Railway, of the superiority of his motivational methodologies in the stimulation of Scruffians as were recalcitrant by vulgar birth, to the task of tunneling, whereby aforesaid Mister Jinkalock professed his convictionalised expectation, through aforesaid Most Illuminating Demonstration, to win the contract for constructional labour on the proposed extension of the City and South London Railway to Islington, the indentured scruffs of his competitors currently working among the navvies being notoriously, to aforesaid competitors' discredit, *shiftless little bastards*.

•

With all that Stamp-tweakery now, it were well into the gloaming, London's lights striking up a sea of gold below, beyond the dark of trees as the Heath rolled down to, a glimmer of gaslights hazed by fog. So as Joey Picaroni ganders down on it, there's a call from Trude.

—Grub's up!

Joey turns back to the campfire, takes the bowl Yapper reaches him. Only… Squirlet takes it right from his hand, don't she?

—No, says she.

Them Scruffians, they'll bounce back to starving, see, as they was Fixed, but if Joey's to pass for a workhouse boy…

•

So poor Joey has to sit and watch them Scruffians tuck in while's his belly rumbles, Yapper mouthing *sorry*, Flashjack scarfing his nosh with gusto, proclaiming it the tastiest ever. Joey minds it a little less, right enough, when he sees Vermintrude adding *schnozzle salt,* as she calls it, to hers— ick! Still, it's a fucker to go to bed on an empty tummy, eh? But Joey took it with the stubbornest scofflaw's grit, so when's they snuggled down that night, why, bugger me if Whelp didn't curl in cosy between Joey and Yapper, like as Picaroni were already pack.

Befores even the crack of dawn, they wakes the next morn, Squirlet poking ribs with her boot, Jake already up and about, harnessing one of the landau's horses to a cart, earning a snorty head toss from a beast as reckons this beneath his station. Flashjack whistles music hall ditties—so chipper as makes Joey mutter murderous grump—but it's Squirlet what Vermintrude wipes the bogies from her eyes to watch, Squirlet studying a blanket of tools and weapons, picking one up every now and then to… just vanish it. It's a trick as don't grow old. Like us, eh?

•

Finally, Eleasar Jinkalock climbs up to the front of the cart, whiles Flashjack and Joey lifts Vermintrude and Squirlet up into the back, then hops up themselves. Down in the dirt, Yapper crouches to Whelp, tells him *sit, stay*, not to follow em, but wait here with these nice folks till Yapper come back for him, and not to bite none of em neither, 'specially not the throats.

Well, that's what he tells him in English, anyways. What he tells Whelp in Dog don't nobody know but Yapper and Whelp, and them tinker's dogs what's all peeping from their tents.

•

Then with a jump to catch a hand, Yapper's heaved up and in by Flashjack, the five's all settled down in back, cross-legged, and Mister Eleasor Jinkalock gives a *hie*, then they's off, the dobbin plodding slow with his solitary burden. Ain't hardly a bird begun to tweet all the way in, nor a milk dray delivering to the Lord Mucks of Marylebone round Regent's Park. Ain't till they reaches Baker Street in the dawn's pale pisslight, the city's first stirrings begin.

Hyde Park, Constitution Hill, Buck House.

Into the valley of death rides the six hungry.

•

Into the City of Westminster, they rides, down by where's the fuckers now has their memorial to Ripper Vicky, golden Victory with her switch, standing proud on a globe, Trade and Conquest kissing her tootsies, one with compass, t'other with club. Round Wellington Barracks and onto

Petty France, they rides, towards the pompous pile of Queen Anne's Mansions. Down Palmer Street, they rides, over the railway, and left onto Caxton, past the grand gated courtyard entrance of an hulking red brick monster, left and left again. Into the lane round back. Into the scruff-trader's entry.

Into the Insititute they goes.

## PART THREE

• 1

Through an arch they goes, into a back court grim as slaughterhouse yard, with loading plinths at doors, stickmen sentrying the entrance Eleasor points his Scruffians at, whacking em off the cart and into single file with his cane: Joey; Yapper; Squirlet; Vermintrude; Flashjack. He marches em to it, flourishing papers, spieling fabbles.

The boss guard eyes the certificates given, then Joey, crooks a finger.
—Open yer shirt.
Joey opens his shirt, edgy as the guard brings out a pocketknife.
—Hand.
He gives his palm to be grabbed, nicked, held and watched as it bleeds.
—Go.
In he's waved.

•

—Next.
Yapper steps forward now, opens his shirt. As he stands there, in his nerves, he almost tugs at the neckerchief, by crikey, almost shows his stitches.
—Hand.
—Good God, man! explodes Jinkalock. There's a reason I'm here at this hour!
And oh how he blusters, bullies: such squandery of his time! for a child as patently has no Stamp! does the fool not know the name of Jinkalock?
And the fool, he does, for Rake Jake Scallion don't do any of his guises by half. So now it's *begging yer pardon, sir,* and *perhaps—yes, sir—very well, sir.*

•

Squirlet next then, scowling at the stickman's gaze as she unbuttons her dress, Jinkalock interrupting, erupting again, at the man's impertinence, such impropriety with his property: would he leer at the girl? strip her bare? and the *child?* hark at her! hark!

For Trude she's busted loose now too, bawling bloody murder, shrieks as splits everyone's ears! Why, the chaos, the cacophony—by the time it's Flashjack stepping up, them stickmen just wants these brats in others' hands, into the breaking cells. Course, there's the fierce grin Flashjack give em besides.

—Go, go, says they. Take em in, sir, please!

• 

Inside, it's like the front of a plod-house, benches round walls, a front desk where's the duty clerk studies them indenture papers, adds his stamps, and scritches everything down in his logbook, peering at em, one by one. Squirlet makes like a sister shushing Trude, takes her hand, meets his snooty look.

—*She's* not got her curse on, sir? Don't want her Fixed in flow.

—Certainly not, sniffs Jinkalock.

Now. The arrangements for collection? First thing Tuesday? Bully!

At the door, Jake stops a moment, looks back. Tips a wink.

The duty clerk taps his brass bell:

*Ting!*

• 2

And it's *Hup to it! Shift!* as two orderlies hustle the scruffs away, down corridors, tiled, to an enormous cage elevator as rattles em down, down, down toward the dungeons. All pressed in tight, they cowers in *terror* of the brutes, so it seems, as one fakes a swipe at em, *hoho!* All pressed in tight, and each of em feels a nudge from Squirlet, things pressed into their hands. A penknife. Letter-opener. Straight razor. You know… the usual.

Buggered if I knows, mate. She's still doing that trick today and still don't *nobody* know where she keeps em.

•

Oh, but them orderlies is having a right old laugh now, one of em joking how's maybe they should steer the waifs by the cell with Himself's pet scruff, show em what's waiting if they gets uppity. Why, the damage they heard done to that uppity punk, while's they was in and out with all of yesterday's fresh meat. How that scruff *squealed* to be clipped!

—Yeah, but he'll have grown em back, won't he? says one.

—Just have to snip em off again, says t'other. And again and again—

—And again? says Flashjack. Cause if yer starting a collection…

• 

Then it's BAM! as Flashjack's bonce smacks the fucker's nose, and POW! as Joey jinks sharp, a roundhouse sucker-punch for the second guard. And Flashjack's hand claps his man's gob, while's Joey's arm locks the other's throat. And here's Squirlet and Yapper on a truncheon hand each, straight razors at tendons, blood spraying everywheres! Trude with a penknife in each fist for pitons, clawing up thighs, up belly, up chest, to throat! It's Flashjack's frenzied spike in a crotch, a blur! It's muffled screams, wild eyes, and something gruesome slithering down a trouser-leg!

It's fucking Scruffian fucking vengeance, mate.

•

I won't say as they made mincemeat of them orderlies, but it weren't far off. Why, them Scruffians was bloodier than bonesaws, wiping weapons and hands on any scrap of tog as wasn't asplatter. Well… OK, Vermintrude being Vermintrude, she were just poking the stinky guts… but yer catches me drift.

Anyways, they's at the dungeons now, so Flashjack hops a corpse, grabs the handle what controls the elevator.

—Take us up, says Squirlet.

But he don't. What he does is heave the door open. Give her a look.

—*Flashjack*, says Squirlet. Jack, what…?

—Puckerscruff, says he.

Then he's offsky.

• 3

So, yeah, as yer can imagine, what come out of Squirlet's mouth then is what yer calls *colourful*, but there ain't no time to go chasing the scallywag, she reckons. Bugger it, let the hellion raise hell down here, see if he can spring his sweetheart, while's they do the *actual job*. So, it's up they go now, Squirlet pulling out a ticker from fuck knows where to check the hour. Hoping Foxtrot's got his runners out, spread the word. Never mind Flashjack; right now *every* Scruffian in the city should be raising hell, drawing the stickmen out. Fingers crossed.

•

Sure enough, it's a quiet floor they comes out in. Well, *relatively* quiet. They was doing experiments by them days, in them labs round the vault, so there was bedlam shrieks to curdle yer very blood, but it were quiet in terms of stickman sentries, like. And Scruffians is sneaky bastards, all's the more so when they's led by one as could hide an elephant behind an hanky. So, slowly but surely, they works their way in, to the heart of the Institute, and they ain't rumbled, they ain't nabbed.

Whassat? Too easy? Well, I *suppose* yer might think that.

•

Now, I ain't gonna milk it like them movies. Weren't no *Whassat?!* then *Phew! It's just a cat!* But there *were* one event to tell.

For here's this orderly in his office, see, ears perked to a sobbing. Out he steps into the corridor: Where's *that* coming from? He follows the creepy crying, round this corner, round that, until why, in the middle of the corridor, there's Vermintrude, a bloody spectre. Hand to his truncheon, he steps forward and…

SSHHEEOOWWHH! Yapper and Squirlet zips behind him, razors slashing hamstrings, and he's down on his knees, Joey at his neck—SNAP!

•

So it weren't like they just waltzed in, mate. No, they left bodies in their wake, stuffed in closets and jiggered elevators. And Joey he were guised up in orderly's whites by the time as they got deep, peachy for ruses as the one they pulls now.

—Aaargh! Joey cries, staggering into the vault's antechamber, clutching his bloody breast. For I am foully murdered!

And he's down, and they runs to him, and Joey grasps em, gasps as they leans over him, pulls em in close…

—Scruffians… he hisses. *STAMP!*

And three Scruffians come belting in, blades swishing, slicing… slaughtering.

• 4

Meanwhiles, of course, Flashjack he's been making his way through the dungeons, melting the wires as runs along the ceiling for the ringing of alarm bells, and more. They says the Devil has a red right hand? Well, Flashjack's, his is white—*white hot*. It ain't a trick as he can fingersnap for fun, but put his darling in a situation, and that hellion's thermite palm will turn an iron lock to liquid, broil a man's balls in his grip, clamp round yer throat and squeeze yer head right off its blooming shoulders. Till he stands afore his Puckerscruff's prison.

•

Course, Flashjack's fiery faculties *might* have come in handy *here*, Squirlet's reckoning right then, as she stands before the great steel safe door of the Stamp's vault. *If* that hand of glory didn't just sputter to a candle flame, or accidentally blow the whole melty door in, destroying everything.

See? Even Flashjack says it's a fair cop.

That's why it weren't the plan anyways. That's why it were Vermintrude up now, scrambling a pile of bodies to reach the lock, a combination lock schemed by the same crafty Kraut what invented such shenanigans… for Tiffany's, no less.

*Too easy?* Ha!

•

As Vermintrude were putting her ear to this door, elsewheres Flashjack were putting his hand to another—which yer has to picture being just one door in an whole long corridor, and that corridor just one passage in an whole horrible warren, and all's the way through it, to where's Flashjack's stood, a trail of bodies and burning. And chanting's coming from them cells now:

—Orphans, foundlings, latchkey kids! Urchins, changelings, live-by-wits!

Cause them cells was full of Scruffians scrobbled for Scrubbing, smelling their liberation.

—*Rascals, scallywags, ruffians, scamps! Scoundrels, hellions, Scruffians STAMP!*

And Flashjack's hand flames white.

• 

And upstairs, in a hushed room, Vermintrude with her ear pressed to cold steel hears a last little click of a tumbler falling into place—she's only done it!

—Bingo! she cries, and: In! Your! Face!

And down she hops from the pile of corpses, what's dragged away now, Joey hauling this one by his arms, Squirlet and Yapper tugging that one by his legs, till's the vault door's clear. Joey grabs the spinny handle, slams it down, whirls it loose. He heaves back with all his might, and that door swings wide.

But the vault's bleedin empty, innit!

• 5

Oh, there's the pedestal what they keeps the Stamp on, alright, bang in the centre of this marble chamber. There's the pedestal stood there as a font in a chapel, a white stone pillar with its capital cushioned in swankiest velvet, red as a postbox or omnibus, red as royal robes, red as blood—yours, mine, or any purple-pissing porphyriac posh cunt's blood, for all's they call it blue. There's even the dent in the cushion where's the Stamp were sat like St Edward's Crown. But there ain't no Stamp there now, not a hide nor hair of it.

•

All's there is, they sees as they enters, Squirlet first, Joey behind her, then Yapper and Vermintrude, is marble-clad floors and walls with alcoves left, right and ahead, a statue skulking in each nook to make yer Templar's Baphomet seem loverly as a music hall cherub. A bull-head this side holds a babe above a brazier. An eagle-head thataways holds its moneybags above a babe. Moloch and Mammon. There's a lion-head on the last, as holds keys in its mitts, a chained child at its feet…

Mithras, what them Romans switched for Scruffian Christ.

•

Gob's honest truth, mate. Fixed at twelve to build them pyramids. It weren't no Flight *into* Egypt, mate. Think on his savvy as a nipper. How else could yer crucify him, and he'd still bounce back?

His message were right Scruffian too, till em Imperial eagles gets their talons in it, twists it all to sin and sacrifice, half-buries it in their own spy's bollocks. And why else is Christmas on their soldier boy's birthday? Oh, that Empire done a right number on his message. Twisted it to justify the very crimes as he cursed, and in his name.

• 

So Squirlet and Joey, Yapper and Vermintrude, they's looking round em in horror, partly to see as how their mission's gone tits-up, partly to see the terrible truth—that the Institute ain't just a business growed with the British Empire, but a monstrous Order as stretches back… fuck knows… *forever?* The Children's Crusade. The Colosseum. The Pyramids.

—We have to leave, says Squirlet. Now.

But that's when there's an horrible rattling clatter and *CLANG!* as a grate come slamming down in the doorway behind them, and they finds themselves stood there, in this dread vault of diabolical idols, trapped.

• 6

—They'll be *fine*, Flashjack is saying that very instant, funny enough. Squirlet's well savvy, says he, and Trude is—ow!

To the dead-arm punch, Puckerscruff adds a flail of slapping for good measure, a lot less grateful to be rescued than Flashjack imagined.

—You had one thing to do, says he. One thing!

He shoves Flashjack into the stairwell.

—The other prisoners…? says Jack.

—The *Stamp*, says Puckerscruff. That's all that matters. And you, our hellion firepower, left one scrag, two scamps and…

He trails off to an exasperated huff.

—Come on, he says. Maybe they ain't Scrubbed yet.

•

So they takes the stairs fast as Puckerscruff's pins can go, legging it for the vault what Flashjack *miraculously* atcherly remembers the location of. But there's stickmen on the landings, in every corridor, round every corner. Ain't nothing that pair can't carve through with fire and spike, but it don't exactly improve Puckerscruff's mood.

—Didn't Foxtrot sort diversionary strikes? he snarls as he pops an eyeball with elbow spike.

—He was s'posed to, shrugs Flashjack as he melts a face.

—Cuntflaps! snaps Puckerscruff.

Flashjack… thinks better of saying how pretty Puck's hair looks, tweaked green by a torturing scalpel's nick.

•

But at last:

—This way! shouts Flashjack, and they's round the final corner, into an hallway stretching before em all the way to—fuck!

For there, at the end of it, beyond the door, in the antechamber of the vault, stands the Waiftaker General square in sight, framed to be seen, staring back at em cold. And before him is his prisoners, Joey and Squirlet on their knees, as brings their bonces to the same height as Yapper and Vermintrude's, all of which has pistols pointed at em by the stickmen at their backs.

—Come join us! calls the Waiftaker General.

•

And Flashjack, he comes sprinting down the hall, a lightning bolt of hellion fury, right hand blazing, even his eyes afire, so set on his target he don't even hear Puckerscruff crying, Wait, Jack! It's a trap!

And as he springs from the doorway—Now! cries the Waiftaker General, and a wire springs up as nearly slices clean through Flashjack's throat, and though the stickmen holding it is brought down by his momentum, they brings Flashjack whiplashing crashing down too. And the other stickmen each side of the door blasts their crossfire killzone, all of em aiming for his head.

• 7

Flashjack rouses gazing up at a great glass dome as belongs roofing some prince's botanical plunder—or some baron's mad laboratory maybe's. *Shite.* Knows where's he is before the order's even barked, before he's heaved upright by chains round neck and wrist, three stickmen each side playing horse-breaker. Puckscruff told Flashjack of the Fixing he don't recall himself, the altar bang in the room's middle. The huge gray millstone, ten foot high, its edge broad as the most barrely chest. Set back in steel mechanics as is hissing and pistoning, turning slowly, speeding up, to grind, to Scrub.

•

—Such punctuality for a scruff! says the Waiftaker General, who stands between the altar for Stamping and the stone for Scrubbing. Why, I was this instant initiating my inquiry to ascertain whom here must embrace their extermination latterly… having witnessed their foolhardy followers's erasure. Which is to say, whomsoever among you is—and what a sneer he gives now!—your leader.

The others stands handcuffed, Flashjack sees, to either side, held by stickmen.

—We can rule out, indubitably, these three.

The Waiftaker General waves an haughty hand at Vermintrude, Squirlet, Puckerscruff.

—The feminine intellect of wench or catamite presiding? Hardly!

•

—This brat then? he spits, coming forward to poke his cane at Yapper—and jerk it away, near tripping a tumble back, as Yapper hits him with not just a bark but a slavery snarly explosion of rabid doggery. Oh, yeah, they all sees the moment of terror before he rallies, smashes that cane across Yapper's face—once! twice!

—Oh, I remember you, he rages, your cur, and all…

He trembles, reins it in.

—But, no. That scheme was Scallion's, I'll wager, not some… mongrel child's. You, then!

He whirls to Flashjack.

—You arsonist, anarchist, assassin and abomination! You *animal!*

•

—No, scorns he. No, if I afforded you the perspicacity of an ape, I might sustain such a conjecture, but the murderous mayhem you have wreaked across my city is savagery baser than heathen Negro or rampaging

Silverback. You have a *tail*, scruff, whether it be perceptible only to God Almighty. A vicious *monkey*, you are; and it's the organ-grinder I seek.

So now's it's Joey the Waiftaker General spins to.

—Leaving us then but one scapegrace, all eliminated barring the eldest and, by no coincidence, I'll hazard, most evidently self-possessed.

Joey, who stands sullen as any scofflaw.

• 8

It's Flashjack who's the first to crack a grin, Squirlet who catches his glinty eyes and snickers, what sets Vermintrude and Yapper off giggling, merry as at a Professor squeaking *Judy, Judy, Judy* through his swazzle. Now Puckerscruff, he just loses it, near to pissing himself. Oh, hark at the Waiftaker General! Ain't he a veritable Sherlock Holmes in his deductive detecting!

The Waiftaker General rounds on em, this way, that. Every way he turns them Scruffians laughs at him.

—What?! he roars. What is this?!

—He ain't even a sodding Scruffian, yer numpty! cackles Puckerscruff. He ain't even Scruffian!

•

I tells yer all, I wish with all me heart I were there to see the Waiftaker General's face. Tell em what it were like, Joey. Tell em.

And he should know, cause he got a right good gander when the cunt come striding up in full fury, rips Joey's shirt open to see there ain't a Stamp on him. Oh, he *howled*, didn't he, Joey? He *howled* to be shown for such a ninny.

Still, it were only moments till he'd found his cool, and then his voice come low:

—Not a Scruffian, says he adrip with spite. *Yet*.

•

And he snaps his fingers, and points his cane, crying, *Ring for the Stamp! The Stamp for this wretch!* And a stickman hops to it, darts to a cord hung on a wall, what he pulls. And it were only Flashjack and Joey didn't flinch from the bell what rung out, only them as weren't struck back to their horriblest memories. Cause Squirlet and Vermintrude, Puckerscruff and Yapper, they all knowed what come with that ringing. And sure enough, as them Scruffians is hauled aside, now they sees the Great Doors open, and into the hall… here comes the Stamp.

• 

What's it look like, mate? Well, not much at all's, really. Yer saw how's Ravewaif and Rebelladonna brung it to this crib stuffed in his backpack. It ain't exactly huge. Ain't even too heavy—till it's on yer chest—for all's it looks like concrete, what with the ash and bone mixed in the clay. Just a fat blank cylinder with an hole through for an axle stick.

What were more of a sight, really, were them poor Scruffians as carried it between them, gussied up as pageboys, each with a spike nailed in his noggin to keep him lobotomised.

• 9

Now the Waiftaker General barks his orders, and he ain't messing round no more. No swaggery gloating from this archvillain. No torturous tosh what's only begging for an hero to turn the tables. No, he's brutal efficiency, cuts straight to business: you men, this one; you men, that one. And it's Flashjack for the Scrubbing right now, the bleeding obvious threat to be dispensed with swiftly, even as Joey's grabbed, his arms pinned so's his handcuffs can be took off, so's his arms can be pulled wide for all's he thrashes, his shirt ripped clear of his pale skin.

•

And it's the others to be prepped for Scrubbing soon as Flashjack's done—biggest to smallest, the waiftaker orders, one by one, and not a second squandered from this scruff to the next. Clockwork! Machinery! Godspeed and Industry! And they fights to bite, they wriggles like crazy, but from scrag to scamp, ain't none a match for em as pins their arms back, rips their togs open, tears away the skin disguising Stamps.

And Joey twists his head to see em struggle, see Flashjack being dragged toward the millstone, as they hauls him and pins him flat on the altar.

•

I can't tell yer how it is, strays. I can't tell yer how it feels to Joey, as them lobotomised Scruffians comes and lays the Stamp on him, and rolls it up over his chest to read his essence, lifting it up at his chin, then lays it back down on him again, and rolls it down to write that essence back into him. I can't tell yer how it was to Joey, nor how it was to me, nor any other Scruffian. I can't tell yer how it will feel to you. Ain't no pain in the world compares.

•

All I can tell yer is that Joey screams as they Fixes him, screams as he ain't never before and never will again, and for all's the seconds Fixing takes, it seems to last forever. Why, it's near unfathomable to Joey, when it's suddenly over, that he can still hear Flashjack cursing, that the hellion ain't even Scrubbed yet.

Then the Waiftaker General's smirking down at him, smug.

Then that fucker ain't smirking no more. For Joey, he's laughing like a madman, not like the others howling at the groanhuff's mistake, but wild, delirious… *triumphant.*

—Look up, says the Scruffian.

## PART FOUR

• 1

—Look up, says Joey Picaroni, and as the Waiftaker General does…

KERSMASH! Through that glass dome above comes crashing the bestest friend Scruffians ever had. It's Rake Jake Scallion to the rescue, high in the sky beyond him the airship what he's jumped from. In he comes, glass shattering at his boots, raining down on everything, with an ivory-gripped, snub-snouted British Bulldog in each hand, courtesy of Mister Philip Webley and Son of Birmingham, unlatching parachute as he drops.

Shusht, Joey. It ain't a fabble if it don't take some liberties.

Well, if yer gonna be like that…

•

KERSMASH! Why, if it ain't Whelp too! And he don't even *needs* a parachute, cause he's the Beast of Buskerville what was Fixed for a cruel schoolboy's pet, and dumped to drown for being Fixed fierce, and chewed his way from his cage, stalked a schoolboy growed to beak-nosed, beady-eyed bastard, turned his hair white, took one bollock, and left him alive only to live in mortal fear of this moment. That Whelp, he's too fucking *ferocious* to even notice the glass shattered by his paws, nor the marble floor as cracks at his landing. He just howls.

•

Cause, yeah, like Foxy would be took in by the Waifstaker General's tricks! Like he'd let his mates just walk into the lion's den, try and steal the Stamp from an empty vault! He knowed that, whether those plans was left out to be stole on purpose or not, them groanhuffs would move the Stamp, knowed that them fuckers would see em coming, set a sneaky trap. But he outhunk em. For weren't it a surefire certainty that the Waiftaker General would Fix any stray what had thrown in with the Scruffians? And *that* would put the Stamp in reach.

•

—Old chap, says Foxy to Joey Picaroni back in his den, I understand you consider yourself… an ally.

And that's when Foxtrot give the stray a choice, just as we did you two, give him the *choice* to take the Stamp. He didn't have to do it. He didn't owe them nothing—why, in helping Yapper and Jake, he weren't even an *interested party*, as they says. But if he were out to strike a blow against the world, they could offer him that chance. For their taking of the Stamp—*his* taking of the Stamp—would make fucking history.

• 2

So it's all for this moment, strays, all for this moment of Rake Jake Scallion with his arms wide as Joey's on the altar, the Webley in each hand spitting point four five five bullets, them puppies with a bite every bit as vicious as their bark: BLAM! BLAM! And two of the guards holding Flashjack falls. BLAM! BLAM! Two more heads is blasted. BLAM! BLAM! The last two drop. So now Flashjack grips the slack chains round his throat with a white hot thermite right hand of glory, and he rips them away like fucking putty. And he turns.

•

Whelp's no sooner on the ground than he's in action too, and blow me if he don't prove himself Scruffian as any twolegs, for it ain't the Waiftaker General he goes for, no, it's the guard what's holding Yapper, duh. You think he's gonna pounce on his revenge, when his best chum's pinned by some stickman begging for his throat to be gnashed?

Besides, Flashjack he's whipping the chains round his wrists out, swinging em past each other as a scissor of steel link what only *just* misses a Waiftaker General diving panicked. Takes out the guards pinning Joey though.

•

On the altar now, Joey snatches them spikes in the bonces of the pageboy Scruffians each side, whips his knees up under the Stamp to his chin, plants his feet on the front of them Scruffians' fancy tunics, and kicks em away to rip the spikes right out their heads. And Joey he ain't got all of Flashjack's acrobatics, but a clown knows how to tumble, so in a trice he's rolled backwards off the altar and landed on his feet. And Joey he ain't got none of Flashjack's hellion tricks, but that don't matter to the first stickman spiked.

• 

And Squirlet and Trude? In the chaos what's erupting they don't even *need* no cavalry to rescue em. Cause the stickmen holding them ain't giving a thought to two *little girlies*, Scruffian or not. So as meaty hands loose collars for clubs, Trude twists and bites, and spits two bloody fingers out; and fuck knows where she sprung em from, but Squirlet has a straight razor in each hand, she's whirling now and slashing em crosswise—swish! swoosh!—to carve an X in a belly. As the entrails spills at Squirlet's feet, Trude's on her stickman's face, thumbs squishing eyes.

• 3

But as the last four bullets from Jake's guns take out the guards holding Puckerscruff, they ain't the only gunshots now. All em stickmen as has guns is firing em now, bullets flying everywhere. And alarms is ringing so's more stickmen are pouring in. Flashjack's chains round stickman necks gets grabbed. Joey's cornered. Puckerscruff's kneecapped. Trude's skull cracks under clubs. And as Squirlet slashes her way to the only thing as matters—the Stamp rolling on the floor where it were dropped by its bearers—bullets batter her back, dance her like a ragdoll. Them stickmen ain't no stormtroopers, mate.

•

The Waiftaker General ain't no snooze neither. He's dived across the floor, beneath the hail of bullets, and now by fuck he's got the Stamp in one arm, scrambles for the doors—but no! Whelp's there before him, blocking his way. He dodges the dog's pounce, swinging his cane—CRACK!—across Whelp's skull, and it don't no more'n irk the dog, and the Stamp goes flying, but his broke cane's now a foot of splinter what he whirls up to meet the dog's next leap, pointed straight into the open jaws, driving straight into Whelp's gob, up into his brain.

•

Yapper comes at him as a fury unleashed. Every one of em Scruffians is a fury unleashed at that. Jake and Joey's plowing a way to the doors, to slam em shut. And Vermintrude, Squirlet, Puckerscruff, they's a swarm of claws and razors and spikes, taking guards down beneath em, one by one. Flashjack's chains are falling molten from his wrists. And oh, he's a dance of death now.

But the Waiftaker General's staggering back toward the millstone, ripping Yapper off him, swinging him through the air, hands clamped on neck and leg, the scamp's chest headed for the grind.

•

Through the slaughter comes Rake Jake Scallion, not a body tripping him, not a bullet hitting him. Through the havoc he comes, so lightning swift as to rival Flashjack as he springs off one foot to spring off the altar with the other, flying through the air, roaring for Yapper. But oh, that villain, mates, that villain, he turns, he sees, and he throws Yapper from him, arching back out of Jake's path, and letting that path take Jake to the stone. And he's thrown himself at Jake's back. He's slamming him into the grind. And it's monstrous, monstrous… monstrous.

• 4

He's gone, mates, he's gone. Rake Jake Scallion, the boldest, bravest, biggest-hearted, belly-laughing best chum as ever wore the Stamp. And don't you dare say he weren't—any of yer. And don't you dare say the fabbles of him tells it larger than life. Why, didn't he jump a hundred feet—two hundred! three!—from a stolen airship, to smash his way into the heart of evil and save the very Scruffians as stole the Stamp? Didn't he, Flashjack? Puckerscruff? Joey?

See? See? You mark it as Joey said it, mates. You mark it. Jake were the best.

•

So can yer imagine it, mates, how's the heroes as were left went wild? How they gawped in horror at empty togs dropping from the Waiftaker General's hands. How the last dozen stickmen in that room glanced to doors as Joey was barring. How they turned their guns on Flashjack, desperately blasting, but he whirled to snatch every bullet, let the molten lead drip as their guns clicked empty. How Yapper yanked the stick from Whelp's gob, chucked it aside. Growled.

How them Scruffians went wild then, butchering, till's the murderer stood alone among em.

How he tried to run.

• 

BOOF! Flashjack dropkicks him in his gut, and the Waiftaker General staggers back and around, folding over double, his mouth an O of exploding breath. BAM! Puckerscruff punches him in the gob, and the Waiftaker General spins round on the spot, that O all squished to one side now. SHERSHWISH! And Squirlet's razors come slicing through the air, across the Waiftaker General's face, slicing that squished O wide as a corpse's grin. CRUNCH! CRACK! And that's Trude and Yapper with stickmen clubs, taking out a kneecap each, and you can't imagine how twisty a grimace that O is now.

• 

SMACK! Even as he's crumpling forward, Joey boots him in the face, kicks him up and over to land flat on his back. And Puckerscruff and Vermintrude leaps for *this*, while's Squirlet and Yapper pounces on *that*, a scamp and scrag on each arm, pinning the bastard down. For all's his legs is busted, though, he tries to kick, so now Flashjack crouches, clamps fiery hands to knees. Burns right fucking through em, he does, leaving only stumps. Then steps aside.

And what's this? Whelp coming slouching in, mate. Sinking his fangs between the thighs. Ripping that cuntfucker's goolies right off.

• 5

So now Flashjack Scarlequin and Whelp stand at his feet—or at the stumps of thigh, at least, where's his feet ought to be. And Joey Picaroni stands at his head looking down on this fucker as deserves all he's got and more, the Waiftaker General shrieking up at him, spitting blood, sobbing for mercy between gasps… or swearing misery? They's all damned, is the gist of it, maybe's. Whatever they does to him can't change that. Joey, he looks at the spikes in his hands what might end the man forever. No. He lets em clatter to the floor.

•

No, he ain't gonna drive em spikes through the man's eyes, into his brain. Instead, Joey kneels, a knee each side of the bastard's head, and he reaches an open palm to Squirlet. Ain't nobody there knows why's they's leaving it to this fresh-Fixed scofflaw as ain't got none of their history. But it just seems right—like the Waiftaker General fingered him for leader, and here's them showing how's they shares even that. So Squirlet puts the straight razor in his hand without's even a word.

Joey flicks it open, draws it slow across the Waiftaker General's throat.

• 

—Let him go, says he as the blood sprays. And they lets him go.

The Waiftaker General clamps his hands to his throat, tries to stem the blood, but it ain't no good. It squirts, spurts. And with every pulse, life spews out between his fingers. And what with his wind kicked out of him by Flashjack, his jaw shattered by Puckerscruff, his shriek raised to a dogwhistle high by Whelp, and his voicebox opened by Joey, he can't say nothing now, just gasps and gawps, just flails and flops, arms weak and limp, a beggar at Death's door.

•

And while's the Waiftaker General does this, Joey he's standing, stepping round to straddle him the other way now, and kneel again. Down to his knees goes Joey again, and now he slips the straight razor under the white silk cravat this dapper toff wears round his neck, stained scarlet now. Joey slices through it and pulls it off, chucks it away. Then he works his way down a shirt what were fresh from the laundry that morning, no doubt, taking his own sweet time to slice the buttons off... one... by one. Finally, he pulls the shirt open.

Ready.

• 6

They all knows what Joey means by it, but it's a knowing as chills even Flashjack as reckons mayhem merry, even Squirlet as judges sentiment a luxury, even vicious little Vermintrude as fights dirtier than a cornered rat. They all looks at them two Scruffian pageboys huddled in a corner, hugging each other, crying over all the horrors they's seen, crying now's their brains is growed back to grasp em. Can any of em... do *this*?

It's Yapper who picks up the fallen axle pole, threads it back through the Stamp, heaves it all up with a hand each end.

•

That Stamp ain't as heavy as the concrete it looks, but it's still a fair burden for a scamp like Yapper. So he stumbles under the bulk of the thing as he humps it forward. He stumbles at it hanging down in front of him, bumping his legs, but Puckerscruff comes darting now to help, to catch an end so's to carry it between em. And at the sight of it angled between a scamp and scrag of different heights—and maybe's at something more—Squirlet steps in, a hand gentle on Yapper's shoulder to take the burden from him.

•

Joey steps up from the Waiftaker General now, up and away, so's the two scrags can bring the Stamp into place. He steps back beside Flashjack, who smiles at him, not his usual cocky motherfucker grin, but proper friendly. Whelp, he comes up beside Yapper, plonks his arse down and nuzzles him to scratch an ear. Vermintrude stands at the Waiftaker General's head.

And Puckerscruff and Squirlet moves in and waits, until's the gasping becomes a gargling, a guttering. Then they lowers the Stamp to the Waiftaker's General chest, rolls it upways for the reading, and downways for the writing.

•

There weren't no scream left in the Waiftaker General, mates. If there were, no doubt he'd have cried out in the agony as every Scruffian's suffered, as you strays is up for tonight, be warned. Ain't none doesn't scream at it... 'cept him as hadn't the life.

Instead, the Waiftaker General just lays on the floor, the last blood pumping from him in a weak spurt, pumping out of him again. And again, and again, and again. He lays there, with his last breath gargling, guttering forever, not dead but dying, that fucker, dying forever and ever and ever amen.

Yer don't needs to know, really, all the gnarlies of em having at the millstone's workings, smashing that monstrous mechanism as Scrubbed Rake Jake Scallion, nor of Flashjack melting the stone itself—not just the metal, but the *stone*—nor of em opening the Great Doors to face the stickmen beyond. All's that really matters is them other doors as was soon flying open, the front doors of the whole Institute itself, flung wide, and all manner of Scruffians and waifs streaming out. Such a sight it was, mates! Scores of em, hundreds of em, *thousands!*

OK, maybe's not thousands.

•

Wish I could say all's Yapper's crib-mates were among em liberated Scruffians—oh, that'd be peachy, wouldn't it?—but it'd be a lie. And a fabbler might fib, but he won't never lie. No, since that night, them stickmen'd had plenty time, so all's Yapper's mates was as Scrubbed as Jake, and it wouldn't be right to pretend as they wasn't.

Still, there was plenty as were only just scrobbled, and out they all streams from the Institute, so many as it seems it won't never end. *Eventually* that stream turns to dribble though. *Eventually*, out comes the seven.

•

With the last of the Scruffians and waifs scarpering out the courtyard gates, back up the front steps of an Institute what's belching black smoke from a shattered glass dome, it's Whelp comes padding out the front door first, sniffing the air and licking his chops. And if yer really wants gnarlies of their exit, yer won't go wrong to picture him clearing their path.

After him then comes Joey with the Stamp, Flashjack at his side, which is how the Stamp has travelled ever since, mate, with a fresh-Fixed scofflaw as courier and a hellion as escort, see?

•

And finally here comes the scrags and scamps, carrying the Waiftaker General's limp, mutilated, guttering flesh between em, his arms flopping out to the sides, Squirlet and Puckerscruff at a shoulder each, Yapper and

Vermintrude each on a stumpy thigh, walking ahead so's, them being short-arses, the fucker was sorta held up for display, like as kiddiewinks going house-to-house, begging, *Penny for the guy!* for Bonfire Night. What might also, if yer absolutely needs it, explain as why them stickmen weren't too obstacley on the way out, all of em shitting themselves to see such a fate.

• 8

Them stickmen weren't the only ones as had fear struck in their hearts by that dread spectacle. They weren't the only ones as went whiter than a ripped prossie to see the Waiftaker General himself brung down to such wretchedness—and Fixed in it, by God, Fixed in it! For that Scruffian Seven—what should've been eight, mates, should've been eight—they walked bold as brass up the middle of Broadway, bold as brass in the light of day, and groanhuffs just ran from em, bleating panicky prayers, leaving carts where's they halted em and swooned ladies where's they fell.

•

That Scruffian Seven as took the Stamp turned right onto Tothill Street, and as they done so, Yapper he takes a deep breath and starts up the Rhyme.
 —*Orphans, foundlings, latchkey kids!*
 Yeah, the Rhyme as they chanted from the cells, mate. What Trude beside him joins in on now.
 —*Urchins, changelings, live-by-wits!*
 And Puckerscruff and Vermintrude too.
 —*Rascals, scallywags, ruffians, scamps!*
 Flashjack too now, even Whelp barking along.
 —*Scoundrels, hellions, Scruffians STAMP!*
 There were only Joey as didn't join in, and only cause he didn't know it. He'd learn it though, he would. As you will too.

•

Better still, before's long they ain't the only ones as is singing. For all's them Scruffians they'd liberated had scarpered every which way, but even as they's legging it, them as hears the Rhyme stops in their tracks, and they turns, comes back.

So as this magnificent marvelous *motherfucking* seven strides out in procession toward Westminster Abbey, now's that Rhyme's sounding out this way, that way, the streets all round ringing as every Scruffian in earshot gathers to the chant. So now Squirlet takes a breath to bellow another warcry.

—Bring out yer chains! she roars. Bring out yer chains!

•

And as the seven what took the Stamp walks death march slow up past the Parliament and Big Ben, death march slow so's to let the chant spread as wildfire through all of Westminster—and beyond even, to Belgravia and Berkeley Square, across the river to Lambeth, through the whole sodding city, even to Foxtrot in Whitechapel—as they carries that Waiftaker General past the Houses of Lords and Commons, from all directions there comes Scruffians with chains, to wrap the broken body of that beak-nosed, beady-eyed blackguard, to wind him as a living mummy in steel bandages.

• 9

He's heavier than any four scamps and scrags can handle by the time they's out onto Westminster Bridge, of course, and one by one, each of our heroes flags, grip slipping, pins wobbling under em. But what's this? One by one, each of em has some other Scruffian hop to it, take the burden from em. Didn't I say there weren't no singular hero in this story, strays? That they was *all* heroes? Well's *every Scruffian in London* took a turn to bear the weight that day. It were *every* Scruffian who held the Waiftaker General high between em, together.

•

And it were every Scruffian's hand on him, from the smallest scamp's paw to the lankiest scofflaw's claw, as raised the Waiftaker General's body high over the balustrade, and sent him over the edge in his chains, dumped him tumbling and splashing down into the filth of the Thames, to sink into the silt and sewage, and lay there till the end of time, Fixed forevers at Death's door, too weak to even struggle, but knowing—oh, yes, knowing, mate—who he were, and where he were, who it were as sent him there, and why for they sent him.

•

And he rots there to this day, he does, strays. The last of the Waiftaker Generals rots there to this day, his Institute brung low as him, for the Stamp were ours now, and for all as they might rebuild the machinery to Scrub us—the machinery what was as much the stickmen as the stone and brass—for all as they might still scheme to wipe us out, they couldn't *make* us any more, to be their slaves. So it brung the whole Trade down, it did, the taking of the Stamp. And never again, we says, never again.

•

So now it's us as has the Stamp, strays, now's we can *offer* it to any waif as wants, as we done yerselves. We don't *gives* it, yer see? From Joey Picaroni on, yer has to *takes* it. And if's we brung yer in from dossing on the streets, told yer the fabbles and offered the choice, it ain't cause we fancies it some wondrous prize for you, savvy?

It's as Joey says, how he were *already* Scruffian inside, didn't *desire* the Stamp as reward.

No, he *knowed* it were already his. Just waiting to be taken.

So...

You ready?